TOM, TOM, THE PIPER'S SON (page 14)

BABY, BABY BUNTING (page 41)

MOTHER GOOSE
NURSERY RHYMES

MOTHER GOOSE
NURSERY RHYMES

Illustrated by Margaret Tarrant

Bounty
Books

First published in 1990 by Ward Lock Limited

This edition published 2005 by Bounty Books,
a division of Octopus Publishing Group Ltd,
2-4 Heron Quays, London E14 4JP

ISBN   0 7573 1097 8
ISBN 13   9780753710975

Printed and bound in Slovenia

MOTHER GOOSE
NURSERY RHYMES

CONTENTS

TOM, TOM, THE PIPER'S SON

Tom, Tom, the piper's son,
Learnt to play when he was young,
But the only tune that he could play
Was "Over the hills and far away";
Over the hills, and a great way off,
And the wind will blow my top-knot off.

Now Tom with his pipe made such a noise,
That he pleased both the girls and boys,
And they stopped to hear him play
"Over the hills and far away".

Tom on his pipe did play with such skill,
That those who heard him could never keep still;
Whenever they heard they began for to dance –
Even pigs on their hind legs would after him prance.

As Dolly was milking her cow one day,
Tom took out his pipe and began for to play;
So Doll and the cow danced "the Cheshire round",
Till the pail was broke, and the milk ran on the
ground.

He met old Dame Trot with a basket of eggs,
He used his pipe and she used her legs;
She danced about till the eggs were all broke,
She began for to fret, but he laughed at the joke.

DOCTOR FOSTER WENT TO GLOUCESTER

Doctor Foster went to Gloucester,
 In a shower of rain;
He stepped in a puddle, up to his middle,
 And never went there again.

GIRLS AND BOYS, COME OUT TO PLAY

Girls and boys, come out to play,
The moon doth shine as bright as day;
Come with a whistle, come with a call,
Come with a good will, or come not at all.

Leave your supper, leave your slate,
And come to your playfellows in the street;
Come with a shout, and come with a bound,
And dance in the moonlight round and round.

Up the ladder, and down the wall,
A halfpenny roll will serve us all;
You'll find milk, and I'll find flour,
And we'll have a pudding in half-an-hour.

OH, WHERE, OH, WHERE
IS MY LITTLE DOG GONE?

Oh, where, oh, where is my little dog gone?
Oh, where, oh, where can he be?
With his ears cut short and his tail cut long,
Oh, where, oh, where is he?

THERE WAS A LITTLE GIRL

There was a little girl
Who wore a little curl,
    Right in the middle of her forehead;
When she was good, she was very, very good,
    And when she was bad, she was horrid.

RING THE BELL

Ring the bell! *(Giving a lock of the hair a pull.)*
Knock at the door! *(Tapping the forehead.)*
Draw the latch! *(Pulling up the nose.)*
And walk in. *(Opening the mouth and putting in the finger.)*

DANCE LITTLE BABY

Dance, little baby, dance up high;
Never mind, baby, mother is nigh.
Crow and caper, caper and crow,
There, little baby, there you go!
Up to the ceiling, down to the ground,
Backwards and forwards, round and round,
Dance, little baby; mother will sing,
With the merry coral – ding, ding, ding!

SNEEZE ON MONDAY

Sneeze on **Monday,** sneeze for danger;
Sneeze on **Tuesday,** kiss a stranger;
Sneeze on **Wednesday,** get a letter;
Sneeze on **Thursday,** something better;
Sneeze on **Friday,** sneeze for sorrow;
Sneeze on **Saturday,**
  see your sweetheart tomorrow.

LITTLE MISS MUFFET

Little Miss Muffet sat on a tuffet,
Eating her curds and whey;
There came a great spider
   and sat down beside her,
And frighten'd Miss Muffet away.

LITTLE MISS MUFFET

SING A SONG OF SIXPENCE

SING A SONG OF SIXPENCE

Sing a Song of Sixpence,
　A pocket full of rye;
Four-and-twenty blackbirds
　Baked in a pie.

When the pie was opened,
　The birds began to sing;
Was not that a dainty dish
　To set before the King?

The King was in the counting-house,
　Counting out his money;
The Queen was in the parlour,
　Eating bread and honey;

The maid was in the garden,
　Hanging out the clothes;
When down came a little bird
　And snapped off her nose!

GOOSEY, GOOSEY, GANDER

Goosey, goosey, gander, whither shall I wander?
Upstairs and downstairs, and in my lady's chamber.
There I met an old man, who would not say his
    prayers,
I took him by the left leg and threw him down the
    stairs.

THE COCK DOTH CROW

The cock doth crow
To let you know
If you be wise
'Tis time to rise.

Early to bed,
Early to rise,
Is the way to be healthy,
Wealthy and wise.

TO MARKET, TO MARKET

To market, to market, to buy a fat pig;
Home again, home again, jiggety-jig.
To market, to market, to buy a fat hog;
Home again, home again, jiggety-jog.

TWINKLE, TWINKLE, LITTLE STAR

Twinkle, twinkle, little star,
How I wonder what you are!
Up above the world so high,
Like a diamond in the sky!

When the blazing sun is gone,
When he nothing shines upon,
Then you show your little light,
Twinkle, twinkle all the night.

Then the traveller in the dark
Thanks you for your little spark.
He could not tell which way to go,
If you did not twinkle so.

In the dark blue sky you keep,
And often through my curtains peep;
For you never shut your eye,
Till the sun is in the sky.

GREEDY JANE

"Pudding *and* pie,"
Said Jane; "O my!"
"Which would you rather?"
Said her father.
"Both," cried Jane,
Quite bold and plain.

THERE WAS AN OLD WOMAN TOSS'D UP IN A BASKET

There was an old woman toss'd up in a basket,
   Ninety times as high as the moon;
Where she was going, I couldn't but ask it,
   For in her hand she carried a broom.

"Old woman, old woman, old woman," quoth I,
"O whither, O whither, O whither so high?"
"To brush the cobwebs off the sky!"
"Shall I go with thee?"
"Ay, by and by."

A FARMER WENT TROTTING

A farmer went trotting
  Upon his grey mare,
    Bumpety, bumpety, bump!
With his daughter behind him
  So rosy and fair,
    Lumpety, lumpety, lump!

A raven cried "Croak!"
  And they all tumbled down,
    Bumpety, bumpety, bump!
The mare broke her knees,
  And the farmer his crown,
    Lumpety, lumpety, lump!

The mischievous raven
  Flew laughing away,
    Bumpety, bumpety, bump!
And vowed he would serve them
  The same the next day,
    Lumpety, lumpety, lump!

BAA, BAA, BLACK SHEEP

Baa, baa, black sheep, have you any wool?
Yes, sir; yes, sir, three bags full:
One for the master, one for the dame,
But none for the little boy who lives down the lane.

ONCE I SAW A LITTLE BIRD

Once I saw a little bird
Come hop, hop, hop;
So I cried, "Little bird,
Will you stop, stop, stop?"
I was going to the window,
To say, "How do you do?"
But he shook his little tail
And far away he flew.

TWO LITTLE DICKEY-BIRDS

Two little dickey-birds sat upon a hill,
One named Jack, the other named Jill.
Fly away, Jack; fly away, Jill;
Come again, Jack; come again, Jill.

THERE WAS AN OLD WOMAN,
AS I'VE HEARD TELL

There was an old woman, as I've heard tell,
She went to market, her eggs for to sell;
She went to market all on a market-day,
And she fell asleep on the king's highway.

There came by a peddler whose name was Stout;
He cut her petticoats all round about;
He cut her petticoats up to the knees,
Which made the old woman to shiver and freeze.

When this little woman first did wake,
She began to shiver and she began to shake;
She began to wonder and she began to cry,
"Oh! deary, deary me, this is none of I!

"But if it be I, as I do hope it be,
I've a little dog at home, and he'll know me;
If it be I, he'll wag his little tail,
And if it be not I, he'll loudly bark and wail."

Home went the little woman all in the dark;
Up got the little dog and he began to bark;
He began to bark, so she began to cry
"Oh! deary, deary me, this is none of I!"

I THINK SO; DON'T YOU?

If many men knew
What many men know,
If many men went
Where many men go,
If many men did
What many men do,
The world would be better –
I think so; don't you?

If muffins and crumpets
Grew all ready toasted,
And sucking pigs ran about
All ready roasted,
And the bushes were covered
With jackets all new,
It would be convenient –
I think so; don't you?

DAVY, DAVY, DUMPLING

Davy, Davy Dumpling,
  Boil him in the pot;
Sugar him and butter him,
  And eat him while he's hot.

JACK A NORY

I'll tell you a story
About Jack a Nory,
And now my story's begun;
I'll tell you another
About Jack and his brother,
And now my story's done.

ON SATURDAY NIGHT

On Saturday night
Shall be all my care
To powder my locks
And curl my hair.
On Sunday morning
My love will come in,
When he will marry me
With a gold ring.

BONNY LASS

Bonny lass, bonny lass,
Wilt thou be mine?
Thou shalt not wash dishes,
Nor yet feed the swine:
But sit on a cushion,
And sew a fine seam,
And thou shalt eat strawberries,
Sugar and cream.

I SAW THREE SHIPS
COME SAILING BY

I saw three ships come sailing by,
Come sailing by, come sailing by;
I saw three ships come sailing by,
   On New Year's Day in the morning.

And what do you think was in them then?
Was in them then, was in them then?
And what do you think was in them then,
   On New Year's Day in the morning?

Three pretty girls were in them then,
Were in them then, were in them then;
Three pretty girls were in them then,
   On New Year's Day in the morning.

And one could whistle, and one could sing,
And one could play on the violin;
Such joy there was at my wedding,
   On New Year's Day in the morning.

I'LL SING YOU A SONG

I'll sing you a song—
Though not very long,
Yet I think it as pretty as any;
    Put your hand in your purse,
    You'll never be worse,
And give the poor singer a penny.

LITTLE GIRL, LITTLE GIRL

Little girl, little girl, where have you been?
Gathering roses to give to the Queen.
Little girl, little girl, what gave she you?
She gave me a diamond as big as my shoe.

TEN LITTLE MICE

Ten little mice sat in a barn to spin,
Pussy came by, and popped her head in:
What are you at, my jolly ten?
We're making coats for gentlemen.
Shall I come in and cut your threads?
No, Miss Puss, you'd bite off our heads.

THE THREE LITTLE KITTENS

Three little kittens they lost their mittens,
  And they began to cry
"Oh, mother dear, we sadly fear
  That we have lost our mittens."
  "Lost your mittens? You naughty kittens!
  Then you shall have no pie!"
    Miaow, miaow, miaow,
    Miaow, miaow, miaow.

Three little kittens they found their mittens,
  And they began to cry
"Oh, mother dear, see here, see here,
  See, we have found our mittens."
  "Found your mittens! You little kittens!
  Then you shall have some pie!"
    Miaow, miaow, miaow,
    Miaow, miaow, miaow,

The three little kittens put on their mittens,
  And soon ate up the pie.
"Oh, mother dear, we sadly fear
  That we have soiled our mittens."

"Soiled your mittens! You naughty kittens!"
Then they began to sigh,
  Miaow, miaow, miaow,
  Miaow, miaow, miaow.

The three little kittens they washed their mittens
  And hung them out to dry.
"Oh, mother dear, look here, look here,
  See, we have washed our mittens!"
"What! Washed your mittens! You darling kittens!
But I smell a rat close by!"
  Miaow, miaow, miaow,
  Miaow, miaow, miaow.

COCK ROBIN GOT UP EARLY

Cock Robin got up early
  At the break of day,
And went to Jenny's window
  To sing a roundelay.

He sang Cock Robin's love
  To pretty Jenny Wren,
And when he got unto the end,
  Then he began again.

THE BARBER SHAVED
THE MASON

The barber shaved the mason,
　　As I suppose
　　Cut off his nose,
And popped it in a basin.

HANDY SPANDY

Handy Spandy, Jack-a-dandy,
Loved plum-cake and sugar candy;
He bought some at a grocer's shop,
And out he came, hop, hop, hop.

TWEEDLEDUM AND
TWEEDLEDEE

Tweedledum and Tweedledee
Agreed to have a battle;
　　For Tweedledum said Tweedledee
　　Had spoiled his nice new rattle.
Just then flew down a monstrous crow,
　　As black as a tar-barrel,
Which frightened both the heroes so,
　　They quite forgot their quarrel.

THE TURTLE-DOVE'S NEST

High up in the pine-tree
  The little Turtle-dove
Made a little nursery,
  To please her little love.
She was gentle, she was soft,
  And her large dark eye
Often turned to her mate,
  Who was sitting close by.

"Coo," said the Turtle-dove,
  "Coo," said she;
"I love thee," said the Turtle-dove.
  "And I love thee."
In the shady branches
  Of the dark pine-tree,
Happy were the Doves
  In their nursery!

The young Turtle-doves
  Never quarrelled in the nest:
They dearly loved each other,
  Though they loved their mother best.
"Coo," said the little Doves,
  "Coo," said she.
So they cooed together kindly
  In the dark pine-tree.

JACK AND JILL

Jack and Jill went up the hill
To fetch a pail of water;
Jack fell down and cracked his crown,
And Jill came tumbling after.

Then up Jack got, and home did trot,
As fast as he could caper.
They put him to bed and plaster'd his head
With vinegar and brown paper.

JACK AND JILL

THREE BLIND MICE

THREE BLIND MICE

Three blind mice, three blind mice,
　　See how they run! See how they run!
They all ran after the farmer's wife,
　　Who cut off their tails with a carving knife.
Did ever you see such a thing in your life
　　As three blind mice?

THE DAUGHTER OF THE FARRIER

The daughter of the farrier
Could find no one to marry her,
    Because she said
    She would not wed
A man who could not carry her.

The foolish girl was wrong enough,
And had to wait quite long enough;
    For as she sat
    She grew so fat
That nobody was strong enough.

THEY THAT WASH ON MONDAY

They that wash on Monday
    Have all the week to dry;
They that wash on Tuesday
    Are not so much awry;
They that wash on Wednesday
    Are not so much to blame;
They that wash on Thursday
    Wash for shame;
They that wash on Friday
    Wash in need;
And they that wash on Saturday,
    Oh! they're lazy indeed.

BABY, BABY BUNTING

Baby, baby bunting,
Daddy's gone a-hunting,
To get a little rabbit's skin
To wrap his Baby Bunting in.

THE PUDDING-STRING

Sing, sing, what shall I sing?
    The cat has eaten the pudding-string!
Do, do, what shall I do?
    The cat has bitten it quite in two.

WHAT DO YOU THINK?

There was an old woman, and what do you think?
She lived upon nothing but victuals and drink;
Victuals and drink were the chief of her diet,
Yet this grumbling old woman could never keep quiet.

THE FAIRY FOLK

Up the airy mountain,
  Down the rushy glen,
We daren't go a-hunting
  For fear of little men;
Wee folk, good folk,
  Trooping all together;
Green jacket, red cap,
  And white owl's feather!

Down along the rocky shore
  Some make their home,
They live on crispy pancakes
  Of yellow tide-foam.
Some in the reeds
  Of the black mountain-lake,
With frogs for their watch-dogs,
  All night awake.

High on the hill-top
  The old king sits;
He is now so old and grey
  He's nigh lost his wits.
With a bridge of white mist
  Columbkille he crosses,

On his stately journeys
   From Slieve League to Rosses;
Or going up with music
   On cold starry nights,
To sup with the Queen
   Of the gay Northern Lights.

They stole little Bridget
   For seven years long
When she came down again
   Her friends were all gone.
They took her lightly back,
   Between the night and morrow;
They thought that she was fast asleep,
   But she was dead with sorrow.
They have kept her ever since
   Deep within the lakes,
On a bed of flag-leaves,
   Watching till she wakes.

By the craggy hill-side,
   Through the mosses bare
They have planted thorn trees
   For pleasure here and there.
Is any man so daring
   To dig up one in spite,
He shall find their sharpest thorns
   In his bed at night.

continued on next page

Up the airy mountain,
    Down the rushy glen,
We daren't go a-hunting
    For fear of little men;
Wee folk, good folk,
    Trooping all together;
Green jacket, red cap,
    And white owl's feather!

William Allingham

IF ALL THE WORLD WAS APPLE PIE

If all the world was apple-pie,
And all the sea was ink,
And all the trees were bread and cheese,
What should we have to drink?
It's enough to make an old man
Scratch his head and think.

LADY-BIRD, LADY-BIRD, FLY AWAY HOME

Lady-bird, lady-bird, fly away home,
Your house is on fire, and your children all gone;
All but one, and her name is Ann,
And she crept under the frying pan.

GERMAN CRADLE-SONG

Sleep, baby, sleep!
Thy father guards the sheep,
Thy mother shakes the dreamland tree,
And from it fall sweet dreams for thee.
Sleep, baby, sleep!
Sleep, baby, sleep!

DIDDLE, DIDDLE, DUMPLING

Diddle, diddle, dumpling, my son John
Went to bed with his trousers on;
One shoe off, the other shoe on;
Diddle, diddle, dumpling, my son John.

IF I WERE AN APPLE

If I were an apple
And grew on a tree,
I think I'd drop down
On a nice boy like me.
I wouldn't stay there
Giving nobody joy;
I'd fall down at once
And say, "Eat me, my boy!"

MISTER FOX, O!

A fox jumped up on a moonlight night,
The stars were shining and all things light;
"Oh, oh!" said the fox, "It's a very fine night
For me to go through the town, heigho!"

The fox, when he came to the farmer's gate,
Whom should he see but the farmer's drake:
"I love you well for your master's sake,
And long to be picking your bones, heigho!"

The grey goose ran right round the haystack:
"Oh, oh!" said the fox, "you are very fat;
You'll do very well to ride on my back,
From this into yonder town, heigho!"

The farmer's wife she jumped out of bed,
And out of the window she popped her head:
"Oh husband, oh husband, the geese are all dead,
For the fox has been through the town, heigho!"

The farmer he loaded his pistol with lead,
And shot the old rogue of a fox through the head;
"Aha!" said the farmer, "I think you're quite dead,
And no more you'll trouble the town, heigho!"

WILLY BOY, WILLY BOY

Willy boy, Willy boy, where are you going?
   I'll go with you, if I may.
I'm going to the meadow to see them a-mowing,
   I'm going to see them make hay.

I WOULD IF I COULD

I would if I could,
If I couldn't how could I?
I couldn't, without I could, could I?
Could you, without you could, could ye?
      Could ye?
      Could ye?
Could you, without you could, could ye?

LEND ME THY MARE

"Lend me thy mare to ride a mile?"
   "She is lamed, leaping over a stile."
   "Alack! and I must keep the fair!
   I'll give thee money for thy mare."
   "Oh! Oh! Say you so?
Money will make the mare to go!"

COME WHEN YOU'RE CALLED

Come when you're called,
    Do as you're bid;
Shut the door after you,
    Never be chid.

SOLOMON GRUNDY

Solomon Grundy,
Born on a Monday,
Christened on Tuesday,
Married on Wednesday,
Took ill on Thursday,
Worse on Friday,
Died on Saturday,
Buried on Sunday.
That was the end
Of Solomon Grundy.

LITTLE TOMMY TITTLEMOUSE

Little Tommy Tittlemouse
Lived in a little house.
He caught fishes
In other men's ditches.

HERE WE GO ROUND THE MULBERRY BUSH

Here we go round the mulberry bush,
The mulberry bush, the mulberry bush,
Here we go round the mulberry bush,
    On a cold and frosty morning.

This is the way we wash our hands,
Wash our hands, wash our hands,
This is the way we wash our hands
    On a cold and frosty morning.

This is the way we wash our clothes,
Wash our clothes, wash our clothes,
This is the way we wash our clothes
    On a cold and frosty morning.

This is the way we go to school,
Go to school, go to school,
This is the way we go to school
    On a cold and frosty morning.

This is the way we come out of school,
Come out of school, come out of school,
This is the way we come out of school
    On a cold and frosty morning.

ELSIE MARLEY

Elsie Marley is grown so fine
She won't get up to feed the swine,
But lies in bed till eight or nine,
And surely she does take her time.

Do you ken Elsie Marley, honey?
The wife who sells the barley honey?
She won't get up to feed her swine,
And do you ken Elsie Marley, honey?

IF ALL THE SEAS WERE ONE SEA

If all the seas were one sea,
What a *great* sea that would be!
And if all the trees were one tree,
What a *great* tree that would be!
And if all the axes were one axe,
What a *great* axe that would be!
And if all the men were one man,
What a *great* man he would be!
And if the *great* man took the *great* axe,
And cut down the *great* tree,
And let it fall into the *great* sea,
What a splish-splash *that* would be!

SWAN, SWAN, OVER THE SEA

Swan, swan, over the sea
Swim, swan, swim!
Swan, swim back again;
Well swam, swan!

GOOSEY, GOOSEY, GANDER

Goosey, Goosey, Gander,
Who stands yonder?
Little Betsy Baker;
Take her up and shake her.

A DOG AND A CAT

A dog and a cat went out together,
To see some friends just out of the town;
Said the cat to the dog,
"What d'ye think of the weather?"
"I think, ma'am, the rain will come down —
But don't be alarmed, for I've an umbrella
That will shelter us both," said this amiable fellow.

ORANGES AND LEMONS

Oranges and lemons,
Say the bells of St. Clement's.

Bull's eyes and targets,
Say the bells of St. Marg'ret's.

Pancakes and fritters,
Say the bells of St. Peter's.

Two sticks and an apple,
Say the bells of Whitechapel.

Halfpence and farthings,
Say the bells of St. Martin's.

When will you pay me?
Say the bells of Old Bailey.

Pray when will that be?
Say the bells of Stepney.

Brickbats and tiles,
Say the bells of St. Giles'.

Kettles and pans,
Say the bells of St. Anne's.

Pokers and tongs,
Say the bells of St. John's.

Old Father Baldpate,
Say the slow bells of Aldgate.

You owe me ten shillings,
Say the bells of St. Helen's.

When I grow rich,
Say the bells of Shoreditch.

I do not know,
Says the great bell of Bow.

Here comes a candle to light you to bed,
Here comes a chopper to chop off your head.

PAT-A-CAKE, PAT-A-CAKE, BAKER'S MAN

Pat-a-cake, pat-a-cake, baker's man!
Make me a cake as fast as you can;
Pat it, and prick it, and mark it with B,
Put it in the oven for Baby and me.

PAT-A-CAKE, PAT-A-CAKE, BAKER'S MAN

HUMPTY DUMPTY

HUMPTY DUMPTY

Humpty Dumpty sat on a wall,
Humpty Dumpty had a great fall;
Not all the king's horses, nor all the king's men
Could put Humpty Dumpty together again.

THE HOUSE THAT JACK BUILT

This is the house that Jack built.
This is the malt
That lay in the house
That Jack built.

This is the rat
That ate the malt
That lay in the house
That Jack built.

This is the cat that killed the rat
That ate the malt
That lay in the house that Jack built.

This is the dog that worried the cat
That killed the rat that ate the malt
That lay in the house that Jack built.

This is the cow with the crumpled horn
That tossed the dog that worried the cat
That killed the rat that ate the malt
That lay in the house that Jack built.

This is the maiden all forlorn
That milked the cow with the crumpled horn
That tossed the dog that worried the cat
That killed the rat that ate the malt
That lay in the house that Jack built.

This is the man all tattered and torn
That kissed the maiden all forlorn
That milked the cow with the crumpled horn
That tossed the dog that worried the cat
That killed the rat that ate the malt
That lay in the house that Jack built.

This is the priest all shaven and shorn
That married the man all tattered and torn
That kissed the maiden all forlorn
That milked the cow with the crumpled horn
That tossed the dog that worried the cat
That killed the rat that ate the malt
That lay in the house that Jack built.

This is the cock that crowed in the morn
That waked the priest all shaven and shorn
That married the man all tattered and torn
That kissed the maiden all forlorn
That milked the cow with the crumpled horn
That tossed the dog that worried the cat
That killed the rat that ate the malt
That lay in the house that Jack built.

This is the farmer that sowed the corn
That fed the cock that crowed in the morn
That waked the priest all shaven and shorn
That married the man all tattered and torn
That kissed the maiden all forlorn
That milked the cow with the crumpled horn
That tossed the dog that worried the cat
That killed the rat that ate the malt
That lay in the house that Jack built.

ALL THINGS BRIGHT AND BEAUTIFUL

All things bright and beautiful,
   All creatures great and small,
All things wise and wonderful,
   The Lord God made them all.

The purple-headed mountain,
   The river running by,
The sunset, and the morning,
   That brightens up the sky;

The cold wind in the winter,
   The pleasant summer sun,
The ripe fruits in the garden,
   He made them every one.

He gave us eyes to see them,
   And lips that we might tell,
How great is God Almighty,
   Who has made all things well.

Cecil Frances Alexander

THE LION AND THE UNICORN

The lion and the unicorn
   Fought for the crown;
The lion beat the unicorn
   Up and down the town.
Some gave them white bread,
   And some gave them brown,
Some gave them plum-cake
   And sent them out of town.

MONDAY'S CHILD IS FAIR OF FACE

Monday's child is fair of face,
Tuesday's child is full of grace,
Wednesday's child is full of woe,
Thursday's child has far to go,
Friday's child is loving and giving,
Saturday's child works hard for its living.
But the child that is born on the **Sabbath Day**
Is bonny, and blithe, and good, and gay.

WHAT ARE LITTLE BOYS MADE OF?

What are little boys made of, made of?
What are little boys made of?
Frogs and snails, and puppy-dogs' tails;
And that's what little boys are made of, made of.

What are little girls made of, made of?
What are little girls made of?
Sugar and spice, and all that's nice;
And that's what little girls are made of, made of.

HOT CROSS BUNS

Hot cross buns! hot cross buns!
One a penny, two a penny,
Hot cross buns!
If you have no daughters
Give them to your sons;
One a penny, two a penny,
Hot cross buns.

SEE-SAW, MARGERY DAW

See-saw, Margery Daw,
    Jacky shall have a new master;
And he shall have but a penny a day,
    Because he can't work any faster.

WHEN THE WIND IS IN THE EAST

When the wind is in the east,
'Tis neither good for man nor beast;
When the wind is in the north,
The skilful fisher goes not forth;
When the wind is in the south,
It blows the bait in the fishes' mouth;
When the wind is in the west,
Then 'tis at the very best.

ST. SWITHIN'S DAY

St. Swithin's Day, if thou dost rain,
For forty days it will remain:
St. Swithin's Day, if thou be fair,
For forty days 'twill rain ne mair.

HE THAT WOULD THRIVE

He that would thrive
    Must rise at five;
    He that hath thriven
    May lie till seven;
And he that by the plough would thrive,
Himself must either hold or drive.

THE GRAND OLD DUKE OF YORK

The grand old Duke of York
He had ten thousand men;
He marched them up to the top of the hill,
Then marched them down again.
And when they were up they were up–up–up
And when they were down they were down–down–
  down
And when they were only half-way up
they were neither up nor down.

HUSH! MY DEAR

Hush! my dear, lie still and slumber;
Holy angels guard thy bed!
Heavenly blessings without number
Gently falling on thy head.

A CHILD'S GRACE

Thank You for the earth so sweet,
Thank You for the things we eat,
Thank You for the birds that sing,
Thank You, God, for everything.

FOR EVERY ILL BENEATH THE SUN

For every ill beneath the sun
There is a cure or there is none.
If there be one, try and find it;
If there be none, never mind it.

SEE A PIN AND PICK IT UP

See a pin and pick it up,
All the day you'll have good luck;
See a pin and let it lay,
Bad luck you'll have all the day.

CHRISTMAS IS COMING

Christmas is coming, the geese are getting fat,
Please to put a penny in the old man's hat;
If you haven't got a penny, a ha'penny will do,
If you haven't got a ha'penny, God bless you.

A WALNUT

There was a little green house,
And in the little green house
There was a little brown house,
And in the little brown house
There was a little yellow house,
And in the little yellow house
There was a little white house,
And in the little white house
There was a little heart.

TWO LEGS SAT UPON THREE LEGS

Two legs sat upon three legs,
With one leg in his lap;
In comes four legs,
Runs away with one leg;
Up jumps two legs,
Catches up three legs,
Throws it after four legs,
And makes him bring back one leg.

One leg is a leg of mutton; two legs, a man;
three legs, a stool; four legs, a dog.

A WELL

Riddle-me, riddle-me, riddle-me-ree,
Perhaps you can tell what this riddle may be:
As deep as a house, as round as a cup,
And all the King's horses cannot draw it up.

GEORGIE PORGIE

Georgie Porgie, pudding and pie,
Kiss'd the girls and made them cry;
When the boys came out to play
Georgie Porgie ran away.

ANN

There was a girl in our towne,
Silk an' satin was her gowne,
Silk an' satin, gold an' velvet,
Guess her name — three times I've tell'd it.

LITTLE BETTY BLUE

Little Betty Blue
    Lost her holiday shoe.
        What can little Betty do?
    Why, give her another
    To match the other,
And then she may walk in two.

SMILING GIRLS, ROSY BOYS

Smiling girls, rosy boys,
    Come and buy my little toys:
Monkeys made of gingerbread,
    And sugar houses painted red.

THERE WAS A JOLLY MILLER

There was a jolly miller
  Lived on the river Dee;
He worked and sang from morn till night,
  No lark so blithe as he.
And this the burden of his song
  For ever used to be—
"I care for nobody—no! not I,
  Since nobody cares for me."

BLOW, WIND, BLOW!

Blow, wind, blow! and go, mill, go!
  That the miller may grind his corn;
  That the baker may take it,
  And into rolls make it,
And bring us some hot in the morn.

JOHN COOK'S LITTLE GREY MARE

John Cook he had a little grey mare
    Hee, haw, hum;
Her legs were long and her back was bare,
    Hee, haw, hum!

John Cook was riding up Shooter's Bank,
    Hee, haw, hum;
The mare she begun to kick and to prank,
    Hee, haw, hum!

John Cook was riding up Shooter's Hill,
    Hee, haw, hum;
His mare fell down and made her will,
    Hee, haw, hum!

The bridle and saddle were laid on the shelf,
    Hee, haw, hum;
If you want any more, you may sing it yourself,
    Hee, haw, hum!

OH DEAR, WHAT CAN THE MATTER BE?

Oh dear, what can the matter be?
Oh dear, what can the matter be?
Oh dear, what can the matter be?
Johnny's so long at the Fair!

LITTLE BO-PEEP

Little Bo-peep has lost her sheep,
   And can't tell where to find them;
Leave them alone and they'll come home,
   And bring their tails behind them.

Little Bo-peep fell fast asleep,
   And dreamt she heard them bleating;
But when she awoke, she found it a joke,
   For they were still a-fleeting.

Then up she took her little crook,
   Determined for to find them;
She found them indeed, but it made her heart bleed,
   For they'd left their tails behind them.

It happened one day, as Bo-peep did stray
   Over a meadow hard by,
That there she espied their tails side by side,
   All hung on a tree to dry.

LITTLE BO-PEEP

ROCK-A-BYE BABY

ROCK-A-BYE BABY

Rock-a-bye baby, on the tree top,
When the wind blows, the cradle will rock,
When the bough bends, the cradle will fall,
Down will come baby, bough, cradle and all.

ONE, TWO, THREE, FOUR, FIVE

One, two, three, four, five,
Catching fishes all alive.
"Why did you let them go?"
"Because they bit my finger so."
"Which finger did they bite?"
"The little finger on the right."

I HAD A LITTLE WIFE

I had a little wife, the prettiest ever seen,
She washed up the dishes and kept the house clean;

She went to the mill to fetch me some flour,
She brought it home safe in less than an hour;

She baked me my bread, she brewed me my ale;
She sat by the fire and told me a tale.

A SWARM OF BEES IN MAY

A swarm of bees in May
Is worth a load of hay;
A swarm of bees in June
Is worth a silver spoon;
A swarm of bees in July
Is not worth a fly.

THERE WAS AN OLD WOMAN
WHO LIVED IN A SHOE

There was an old woman who lived in a shoe;
She had so many children she didn't know what to do.
She gave them some broth without any bread;
Then kissed them all soundly and put them to bed.

THE MAN IN THE MOON

The man in the moon
Came tumbling down,
And asked his way to Norwich:
He went by the south,
And burnt his mouth
With supping cold pease porridge.

LONDON BRIDGE IS BROKEN DOWN

London Bridge is broken down,
    Dance o'er my Lady Lee;
London Bridge is broken down,
    With a gay lady.

How shall we build it up again?
    Dance o'er my Lady Lee;
How shall we build it up again?
    With a gay lady.

Build it up with silver and gold,
    Dance o'er my Lady Lee;
Build it up with silver and gold,
    With a gay lady.

Silver and gold will be stole away,
    Dance o'er my Lady Lee;
Silver and gold will be stole away,
    With a gay lady.

Build it up with iron and steel,
    Dance o'er my Lady Lee;
Build it up with iron and steel,
    With a gay lady.

Iron and steel will bend and break,
    Dance o'er my Lady Lee;
Iron and steel will bend and break,
    With a gay lady.

Build it up with wood and clay,
    Dance o'er my Lady Lee;
Build it up with wood and clay,
    With a gay lady.

Wood and clay will wash away,
    Dance o'er my Lady Lee;
Wood and clay will wash away,
    With a gay lady.

Build it up with stone so strong,
    Dance o'er my Lady Lee;
Huzza! 'twill last for ages long,
    With a gay lady.

AN EGG

In marble walls as white as milk,
Lined with a skin as soft as silk,
Within a fountain, crystal clear,
A golden apple doth appear.
No doors there are to this stronghold.
Yet thieves break in and steal the gold.

COBBLER, COBBLER, MEND MY SHOE

Cobbler, cobbler, mend my shoe:
Get it done by half-past two;
Do it neat, and do it strong.
I will pay you when it's done.

THE ROSE IS RED

The rose is red,
The violet blue;
Honey is sweet
And so are you.

WHEN GOOD KING ARTHUR
RULED THIS LAND

When good King Arthur ruled this land,
   He was a goodly king;
He took three pecks of barley meal,
   To make a bag-pudding.

A bag-pudding the King did make,
   And stuffed it well with plums,
And in it put two lumps of fat,
   As big as my two thumbs.

The King and Queen did eat thereof,
   And noblemen beside;
And what they could not eat at night
   The Queen next morning fried.

COCK-A-DOODLE-DOO!

Cock-a-doodle-doo!
My dame has lost her shoe;
My master's lost his fiddling-stick,
And don't know what to do.

Cock-a-doodle-doo!
What is my dame to do?
Till master finds his fiddling-stick
She'll dance without her shoe.

Cock-a-doodle-doo!
My dame has lost her shoe,
And master's found his fiddling-stick,
Sing doodle doodle doo!

Cock-a-doodle-doo!
My dame will dance with you,
While master fiddles his fiddling-stick,
For dame and doodle doo.

Cock-a-doodle-doo!
Dame has lost her shoe;
Gone to bed and scratched her head,
And can't tell what to do.

HARK, HARK!
THE DOGS DO BARK

Hark! hark! the dogs do bark;
    The beggars are coming to town:
Some in jags, and some in rags,
    And some in velvet gown.

THE FAIR MAID WHO,
THE FIRST OF MAY

The fair maid who, the first of May,
Goes to the fields at break of day,
And washes in dew from the hawthorn tree,
Will ever after handsome be.

THE CUCKOO'S A FINE BIRD

The cuckoo's a fine bird,
He sings as he flies;
He brings us good tidings
He tells us no lies.

PETER PIPER

Peter Piper picked a peck of pickled pepper;
A peck of pickled pepper Peter Piper picked;
If Peter Piper picked a peck of pickled pepper,
Where's the peck of pickled pepper Peter Piper
    picked?

BOW-WOW, SAYS THE DOG

Bow-wow, says the dog;
    Mew, mew, says the cat;
Grunt, grunt, goes the hog;
    And squeak, says the rat.

Tu-whu, says the owl;
    Caw, caw, says the crow;
Quack, quack, goes the duck;
    And moo, says the cow.

ROSEMARY GREEN

Rosemary green
    And lavender blue,
Thyme and sweet marjoram,
    Hyssop and rue.

THIS IS THE WAY THE LADIES RIDE

This is the way the ladies ride:
Tri, tre, tre, tree,
Tri, tre, tre, tree!
This is the way the ladies ride:
Tri, tre, tre, tre, tri-tre-tre-tree!

This is the way the gentlemen ride:
Gallop-a-trot,
Gallop-a-trot!
This is the way the gentlemen ride:
Gallop-a-gallop-a-trot!

This is the way the farmers ride:
Hobbledy-hoy!
Hobbledy-hoy!
This is the way the farmers ride:
Hobbledy hobbledy-hoy!

THREE WISE MEN OF GOTHAM

Three wise men of Gotham
Went to sea in a bowl;
And if the bowl had been stronger,
My song would have been longer.

DANCE TO YOUR DADDY

Dance to your daddy,
My little babby;
Dance to your daddy,
    My little lamb.

You shall have a fishy,
In a little dishy;
You shall have a fishy,
    When the boat comes in.

LITTLE POLLY FLINDERS

Little Polly Flinders
Sat among the cinders,
Warming her pretty little toes!
Her mother came and caught her
And scolded her little daughter,
For spoiling her nice new clothes.

MOLLY AND I

Molly, my sister, and I fell out,
And what do you think it was all about?
She loved coffee, and I loved tea;
And that was the reason we couldn't agree.

UP STREET, AND DOWN STREET

Up street, and down street,
　　Each window's made of glass;
If you go to Tommy Tickler's house
　　You'll find a pretty lass.

WHEN I WAS A LITTLE BOY

When I was a little boy
　　I had but little wit;
It is some time ago,
　　And I've no more yet;
Nor ever, ever shall
　　Until that I die,
For the longer I live
　　The more fool am I.

HUSH-A-BYE, BABY

Hush-a-bye, baby, thy cradle is green;
Father's a nobleman, mother's a queen;
And Betty's a lady, and wears a gold ring,
And Johnny's a drummer, and drums for the King.

"WHERE ARE YOU GOING TO, MY PRETTY MAID?"

"Where are you going to, my pretty maid?"
"I'm going a-milking, sir," she said.

"May I go with you, my pretty maid?"
"You're kindly welcome, sir," she said.

"What is your father, my pretty maid?"
"My father's a farmer, sir," she said.

"What is your fortune, my pretty maid?"
"My face is my fortune, sir," she said.

'Then I can't marry you, my pretty maid!"
"Nobody asked you, sir!" she said.

AS I WAS GOING TO ST. IVES

As I was going to St. Ives,
    I met a man with **seven** wives,
    Every wife had **seven** sacks,
    Every sack had **seven** cats,
    Every cat had **seven** kits:
    Kits, cats, sacks, and wives,
How many were there going to St. Ives?

THE CANARY

Mary had a little bird,
    With feathers bright and yellow,
Slender legs – upon my word,
    He was a pretty fellow!

Sweetest notes he always sung,
    Which much delighted Mary;
Often where his cage was hung,
    She sat to hear Canary.

Crumbs of bread and dainty seeds
    She carried to him daily,
Seeking for the early weeds,
    She decked his palace gaily.

This, my little readers, learn,
    And ever practice duly;
Songs and smiles of love return
    To friends who love you truly.

Elizabeth Turner

WEE WILLIE WINKIE

Wee Willie Winkie runs through the town,
Upstairs and downstairs in his night-gown,
Tapping at the window, crying through the lock,
"Are the children in their beds,
It's past eight o'clock?"

"Hey! Willie Winkie,
Are you coming then?
The cat's singing purrie
To the sleeping hen;
The dog is lying on the floor
And does not even peep;
But here's a wakeful laddie
That will not fall asleep,"

WEE WILLIE WINKIE

POLLY, PUT THE KETTLE ON

POLLY, PUT THE KETTLE ON

Polly, put the kettle on,
Polly, put the kettle on,
Polly, put the kettle on,
We'll all have tea.

Sukey, take it off again,
Sukey, take it off again,
Sukey, take it off again,
They've all gone away.

PARSLEY, SAGE, ROSEMARY AND THYME

Can you make me a cambric shirt,
   Parsley, sage, rosemary and thyme,
Without any seam or needlework?
   And you shall be a true lover of mine.

Can you wash it in yonder well,
   Parsley, sage, rosemary and thyme,
Which never sprung water, nor rain ever fell?
   And you shall be a true lover of mine.

Can you dry it on yonder thorn,
   Parsley, sage, rosemary and thyme,
Which never bore blossom since Adam was born?
   And you shall be a true lover of mine.

Now you have asked me questions three,
   Parsley, sage, rosemary and thyme,
I hope you'll answer as many for me,
   And you shall be a true lover of mine.

Can you find me an acre of land,
    Parsley, sage, rosemary and thyme,
Between the salt water and the sea-sand?
    And you shall be a true lover of mine.

Can you plough it with a ram's horn,
    Parsley, sage, rosemary and thyme,
And sow it all over with one peppercorn?
    And you shall be a true lover of mine.

Can you reap it with a sickle of leather,
    Parsley, sage, rosemary and thyme,
And bind it up with a peacock's feather?
    And you shall be a true lover of mine.

When you have done and finished your work,
    Parsley, sage, rosemary and thyme,
Then come to me for your cambric shirt,
    And you shall be a true lover of mine.

THE VULTURE

The Vulture eats between his meals
    And that's the reason why
He very, very rarely feels
    As well as you and I.

His eye is dull, his head is bald,
    His neck is growing thinner.
Oh! what a lesson for us all
    To only eat at dinner!

I SAW A SHIP A-SAILING

I saw a ship a-sailing,
    A-sailing on the sea;
And, oh! it was all laden
    With pretty things for thee!

There were comfits in the cabin,
    And apples in the hold;
The sails were all of silk,
    And the masts were made of gold.

TO BED, TO BED

"To bed, to bed," says Sleepy-head;
  "Let's stay awhile," says Slow;
"Put the pot on,"
  Says Greedy John,
"We'll sup before we go."

POP GOES THE WEASEL

Half a pound of tuppenny rice,
Half a pound of treacle;
That's the way the money goes—
Pop goes the weasel!

PUSSY-CAT, PUSSY-CAT

Pussy-cat, pussy-cat, where have you been?
I've been to London to see the Queen.
Pussy-cat, pussy-cat, what did you there?
I caught a little mouse under her chair.

YANKEE DOODLE

Yankee doodle came to town,
Upon a little pony,
He stuck a feather in his cap
And called it macaroni.
   Yankee doodle, doodle-doo,
   Yankee doodle dandy;
   All the lassies are so smart,
   And sweet as sugar candy.

Marching in and marching out,
And marching round the town, O!
Here there comes a regiment
With Captain Thomas Brown, O!
   Yankee doodle, doodle-doo,
   Yankee doodle dandy;
   All the lassies are so smart,
   And sweet as sugar candy.

Yankee doodle is a tune
That comes in mighty handy;
The enemy all runs away
At Yankee doodle dandy.
   Yankee doodle, doodle-doo,
   Yankee doodle dandy;
   All the lassies are so smart,
   And sweet as sugar candy.

THE MAN IN THE WILDERNESS

The man in the wilderness asked me
How many strawberries grew in the sea.
I answered him, as I thought good,
"As many herrings as grow in the wood."

IF I HAD A PONY

If I had a pony and he would not go,
Do you think I'd whip him? No, no, no!
I'd put him in the stable and give him some corn,
The best little pony that ever was born!

FRIDAY NIGHT'S DREAM

Friday night's dream
On the Saturday told
Is sure to come true,
Be it never so old.

PETER, PETER, PUMPKIN EATER

Peter, Peter, pumpkin eater,
Had a wife and couldn't keep her:
He put her in a pumpkin shell,
And there he kept her very well.

Peter, Peter, pumpkin eater,
Had another, but didn't love her.
Peter learnt to read and spell
And then he loved her very well.

A CAT CAME FIDDLING OUT OF A BARN

A cat came fiddling out of a barn,
With a pair of bagpipes under her arm;
She could sing nothing but fiddle-de-dee,
The mouse has married the humble-bee;
Pipe, cat–dance, mouse–
We'll have a wedding at our good house.

I HAD A LITTLE PONY

I had a little pony,
  His name was Dapple Gray,
I lent him to a lady,
  To ride a mile away.

She whipped him, she lashed him,
  She rode him through the mire:
I wouldn't lend my pony now
  For all the lady's hire.

LAVENDER'S BLUE

Lavender's blue, dilly, dilly, lavender's green;
When I am king, dilly, dilly, you shall be queen;
Call up your men, dilly, dilly, set them to work:
Some to the plough, dilly, dilly, some to the cart,
Some to make hay, dilly, dilly, some to thresh corn;
Whilst you and I, dilly, dilly, keep ourselves warm.

MASTER RIDDLE-ME-ROO

Master Riddle-me-Roo,
If I've heard true,
Was the strangest fellow
That ever I knew,
He asked for a thrashing
To keep him awake,
And said he liked physic
Better than cake.

He'd run out undressed
In the snow and the ice;
He ate up a thistle
And said it was nice;
He sat on the chimney
Until he fell through;
And that's all I know
Of young Riddle-me-Roo.

LITTLE ROBIN REDBREAST

Little Robin Redbreast
    Sat upon a rail;
Niddle-naddle went his head,
    Wiggle-waggle went his tail.

IF "IFS" and "ANS"

If "ifs" and "ans"
Were pots and pans,
There'd be no need for tinkers!

CURRANTS

Higgledy, piggledy,
Here we lie,
Picked and plucked
And put in a pie.
My first in snapping, snarling, growling,
My second's busy, romping and prowling.
Higgledy piggledy,
Here we lie,
Picked and plucked
And put in a pie.

LEG OVER LEG

Leg over leg,
As the dog went to Dover;
When he came to a stile
Hop! he went over.

THERE WAS A FROG LIVED IN A WELL

There was a frog lived in a well,
  Kitty alone, Kitty alone;
There was a frog lived in a well;
  Kitty alone and I!

There was a frog lived in a well,
And a merry mouse in a mill.
  Cock me cary, Kitty alone,
  Kitty alone and I.

This frog he would a-wooing ride,
  Kitty alone, Kitty alone;
This frog he would a-wooing ride,
And on a snail he got astride,
  Cock me cary, Kitty alone,
  Kitty alone and I.

He rode till he came to my Lady Mouse Hall,
  Kitty alone, Kitty alone;
He rode till he came to my Lady Mouse Hall,
And there he did both knock and call.
  Cock me cary, Kitty alone,
  Kitty alone and I.

Quoth he, "Miss Mouse, I'm come to thee,"—
  Kitty alone, Kitty alone;
Quoth he, "Miss Mouse, I'm come to thee.
To see if thou canst fancy me."
  Cock me cary, Kitty alone,
  Kitty alone and I.

Quoth she, "Answer I'll give you none,"—
  Kitty alone, Kitty alone;
Quoth she, "Answer I'll give you none
Until my Uncle Rat comes home."
  Cock me cary, Kitty alone,
  Kitty alone and I.

The frog he came whistling through the brook,
  Kitty alone, Kitty alone;
The frog he came whistling through the brook,
And there he met with a dainty duck.
  Cock me cary, Kitty alone,
  Kitty alone and I.

This duck she swallowed him up with a pluck,
  Kitty alone, Kitty alone;
This duck she swallowed him up with a pluck,
So there's an end of my history-book.
  Cock me cary, Kitty alone,
  Kitty alone and I.

HOURS OF SLEEP

Nature needs but five,
Custom gives thee seven,
Laziness takes nine,
And Wickedness eleven!

A STAR

I have a little sister,
They call her Peep, Peep,
She wades in the waters,
Deep, deep, deep;
She climbs up the mountains
High, high, high:
My poor little sister,
She has but one eye!

PETER WHITE

Peter White will ne'er go right;
Would you know the reason why?
He follows his nose where'er he goes,
And that stands all awry.

FOR WANT OF A NAIL, THE SHOE WAS LOST

For want of a nail, the shoe was lost,
For want of the shoe, the horse was lost,
For want of the horse, the rider was lost,
For want of the rider, the battle was lost,
For want of the battle, the kingdom was lost,
And all for the want of a horseshoe nail!

THE SQUIRREL

The winds they did blow,
　　The leaves they did wag;
Along came a beggar-boy,
　　And put me in his bag.

He took me up to London:
　　A lady did me buy;
Put me in a silver cage,
　　And hung me up on high.

With apples by the fire,
　　And nuts for to crack:
Besides a little feather-bed
　　To rest my little back.

RIDE A COCK-HORSE TO BANBURY CROSS

Ride a cock-horse to Banbury Cross,
To see a fine lady upon a white horse;
With rings on her fingers and bells on her toes,
She shall have music wherever she goes.

RIDE A COCK-HORSE TO BANBURY CROSS

LITTLE TOM TUCKER

LITTLE TOM TUCKER

Little Tom Tucker, sing for your supper.
What shall he sing for? Brown bread and butter.
How shall he cut it without any knife?
How shall he marry without any wife?

HIGH DIDDLE DOUBT

High diddle doubt, my candle's out,
    My little maid's not at home;
Saddle my hog and bridle my dog,
    And fetch my little maid home.

BIRDS OF A FEATHER

Birds of a feather flock together,
    And so will pigs and swine;
Rats and mice will have their choice,
    And so will I have mine.

FINGERNAILS

Cut them on **Monday,** you cut them for health;
Cut them on **Tuesday,** you cut them for wealth;
Cut them on **Wednesday,** you cut them for news;
Cut them on **Thursday,** a new pair of shoes;
Cut them on **Friday,** you cut them for sorrow;
Cut them on **Saturday,** see your true love tomorrow;
Cut them on **Sunday**, ill-luck will be with you all the
    week.

THE BAKER'S REPLY
TO THE NEEDLE PEDLER

I need not your needles, they're needless to me;
For kneading of needles were needless, you see;
But did my neat trousers but need to be kneed,
I then should have need of your needles indeed.

IF I'D AS MUCH MONEY

If I'd as much money as I could tell,
  I never would cry, "Young lambs to sell,
  Young lambs to sell, young lambs to sell";
  I never would cry, "Young lambs to sell."

I HAD A LITTLE COW

I had a little cow;
Hey-diddle, ho-diddle!
I had a little cow, and it had a little calf,
Hey-diddle, ho-diddle; and there's my song half!

I had a little cow;
Hey-diddle, ho-diddle!
I had a little cow, and I drove it to the stall;
Hey-diddle, ho-diddle; and there's my song all!

THERE WAS A LITTLE MAN

There was a little man, and he had a little gun,
   And his bullets were made of lead, lead, lead;
He went to the brook, and saw a little duck,
   And shot it through the head, head, head.

He carried it home to his old wife Joan,
   And bade her a fire to make, make, make;
To roast the little duck, while he went to the brook,
   To shoot and kill the drake, drake, drake.

   The little drake was swimming,
   With his little curly tail,
And the little man made it his mark, mark, mark:
   He let off his gun,
   But he fired too soon,
And away flew the drake with a quack, quack, quack.

WHEN I WAS A LITTLE BOY

When I was a little boy
I lived by myself,
And all the bread and cheese I got
I put upon a shelf.

The rats and the mice
They led me such a life,
I was forced to go to London
To get myself a wife.

The roads were so bad,
And the lanes were so narrow,
I could not get my wife home
Without a wheelbarrow.

The wheelbarrow broke,
And my wife had a fall;
Down came the wheelbarrow,
Wife and all.

OLD FARMER GILES

Old Farmer Giles
He went seven miles,
With his faithful dog, Old Rover;
And old Farmer Giles,
When he came to the stiles,
Took a run and jumped clean over.

THE SPIDER AND THE FLY

"Will you walk into my parlour?"
 Said the spider to the fly;
" 'Tis the prettiest little parlour
 That ever you did spy.
The way into my parlour
 Is up a winding stair;
And I have many curious things
 To show you when you're there."
"Oh, no, no," said the little fly;
 "To ask me is in vain;
For who goes up your winding stair
 Can ne'er come down again."

"I'm sure you must be weary, dear,
 With soaring up so high;
Will you rest upon my little bed?"
 Said the spider to the fly.
"There are pretty curtains all around,
 The sheets are fine and thin,
And if you want to rest awhile,
 I'll snugly tuck you in!"
"Oh, no, no," said the little fly;
 "For I've often heard it said,
They never, never wake again
 Who sleep upon your bed!"

Said the cunning spider to the fly,–
  "Dear friend, what can I do
To prove the warm affection
    I've always felt for you?
I have within my pantry
  Good store of all that's nice;
I'm sure you're very welcome–
    Will you please to take a slice?"
"Oh, no, no," said the little fly,
  "Kind sir, that cannot be;
I've heard what's in your pantry,
    And I do not wish to see!"

    "Sweet creature!" said the spider,
      "You're witty and you're wise;
    How handsome are your gauzy wings,
      How brilliant are your eyes!
      I have a little looking-glass
      Upon my parlour shelf;
    If you'll step in one moment, dear,
      You shall behold yourself."
    "I thank you, gentle sir," she said,
      "For what you're pleased to say,
    And, bidding you good-morning now,
      I'll call another day."

continued on next page

The spider turned him round about,
　　And went into his den,
　　For well he knew the silly fly
　　　　Would soon come back again.
So he wove a subtle web
　　In a little corner sly,
　　And set his table ready
　　　　To dine upon the fly.

Then he came out to his door again,
　　And merrily did sing,
"Come hither, hither, pretty fly,
　　With the pearl and silver wing;

Your robes are green and purple,
　　There's a crest upon your head;
Your eyes are like the diamond bright,
　　But mine are dull as lead!"

　　Alas! alas! how very soon
　　　　This silly little fly,
　　Hearing his wily, flattering words,
　　　　Came slowly flitting by!
　　With buzzing wings she hung aloft,
　　　　Then near and nearer drew,
　　Thinking only of her brilliant eyes,
　　　　And green and purple hue—

Thinking only of her crested head–
    Poor foolish thing! At last
Up jumped the cunning spider,
    And fiercely held her fast.
He dragged her up his winding stair,
    Into his dismal den;
Within his little parlour,–
    But she ne'er came out again!

And now, dear little children
    Who may this story read,
To idle, silly, flattering words,
    I pray you ne'er give heed;
Unto an evil counsellor
    Close heart and ear and eye,
And take a lesson from this tale
    Of the Spider and the Fly.

CLAP HANDS, CLAP HANDS

Clap hands, clap hands,
Till father comes home;
For father's got money,
But mother's got none.
Clap hands, clap hands,
Till father comes home!

I LOVE SIXPENCE

I love sixpence, pretty little sixpence,
I love sixpence better than my life;
I spent a penny of it, I lent a penny of it,
And then took fourpence home to my wife.

Oh, my little fourpence, pretty little fourpence,
I love fourpence better than my life;
I spent a penny of it, I lent a penny of it,
And then took twopence home to my wife.

Oh, my little twopence, my pretty little twopence,
I love twopence better than my life;
I spent a penny of it, I lent a penny of it,
And then took nothing home to my wife.

Oh, my little nothing, my pretty little nothing,
What will nothing buy for my wife?
I have nothing, I spend nothing,
I love nothing better than my wife.

THERE WAS A PIPER

There was a piper, he'd a cow,
  And he'd no hay to give her;
He took his pipes and played a tune,
  Consider, old cow, consider!

The cow considered very well,
  For she gave the piper a penny,
That he might play the tune again,
  Of "Corn-rigs are bonnie!"

A LITTLE BOY AND A LITTLE GIRL

A little boy and a little girl
  Lived in an alley;
Said the little boy to the little girl,
  "Shall I? oh! shall I?"

Said the little girl to the little boy,
  "What will you do?"
Said the little boy to the little girl,
  "I will kiss you."

W-O-O-O-O-OWW!

Away in the forest, all darksome and
    deep,
The Wolves went a-hunting when men were
     asleep:
And the cunning Old Wolves were so patient
    and wise,
As they taught the young Cubs how to see
    with their eyes,
How to smell with their noses and hear with
    their ears,
And what a Wolf hunts for and what a Wolf
    fears.
Of danger they warned: "Cubs, you mustn't
    go there–
It's the home of the Grizzily-izzily Bear!
     W-o-o-o-o-oww!"

The Cubs in the Pack very soon understood
If they followed the Wolf Law the hunting
    was good,
And Old Wolves who'd hunted long winters
    ago
Knew better than they did the right way to go.
But one silly Cub thought he always was
    right,
And he settled to do his *own* hunting one
    night.
He laughed at the warning–said *he* didn't
    care.
For the Grizzily-izzily-izzily Bear!
     W-o-o-o-o-oww!

So, when all his elders were hot on the track,
"I'm off now!" he barked to the Cubs of the
    Pack.
"I'll have some adventures – don't mind what
    you say!"
A wave of his paw – and he bounded away.
He bounded away till he came very soon,
Where the edge of the forest lay white in the
    moon,
To what he'd been warned of – that terrible
    lair –
The haunt of the Grizzily-izzily Bear!
        W-o-o-o-o-oww!

He came . . . . And what happened? Alas, to
    the Pack
That poor silly Wolf-Cub has never won back.
And once, in a neat little heap on the ground,
The end of a tail and a whisker were found,
Some fur, and a nose-tip, a bristle or two,
And the kindly Old Wolves shook their heads,
    for they knew
It was all of his nice little feast he could
    spare –
That Grizzily-izzily-izzily Bear!
        W-o-o-o-o-oww!

                                    Nancy M. Hayes

AS I WAS GOING TO DERBY

As I was going to Derby,
Upon a market day,
I met the finest sheep, sir,
That ever was fed on hay.

This sheep was fat behind, sir,
This sheep was fat before,
This sheep was ten yards high, sir,
Indeed he could have been more!

The wool upon his back, sir,
Reached up into the sky,
The eagles built their nests there,
For I heard the young ones cry.

This sheep had four legs to walk upon,
This sheep had four legs to stand,
And every leg he had, sir,
Stood on an acre of land.

Now the man who fed the sheep, sir,
He fed him twice a day,
And each time he fed him, sir,
He ate a rick of hay.

DOWN IN YONDER MEADOW

Down in yonder meadow where the green grass
   grows,
  Pretty Polly Petticoat bleaches her clothes.
She sang, she sang, she sang, oh, so sweet,
  She sang, "Oh, come over," across the street.

He kissed her, he kissed her, he bought her a gown,
  A gown of rich crimson to wear in the town.
He bought her a gown and a guinea gold ring,
  A guinea, a guinea, a guinea gold ring.

Up street, and down, shine the windows made of
   glass,
  Oh, isn't Polly Petticoat a pretty young lass?
Cherries in her cheeks, and ringlets in her hair,
  Hear her singing sweetly up and down the stair.

HEY, DIDDLE, DIDDLE

Hey, diddle, diddle, the cat and the fiddle,
  The cow jumped over the moon;
The little dog laughed to see such sport,
  While the dish ran away with the spoon.

HEY, DIDDLE, DIDDLE

HICKORY, DICKORY, DOCK

HICKORY, DICKORY, DOCK

Hickory, Dickory, Dock,
The mouse ran up the clock;
The clock struck one,
The mouse ran down;
Hickory, Dickory, Dock.

THE NORTH WIND

The north wind doth blow,
  And we shall have snow,
And what will poor robin do then,
  Poor thing?

He'll sit in the barn,
  And keep himself warm,
And hide his head under his wing,
  Poor thing!

The north wind doth blow,
  And we shall have snow,
And what will the swallow do then,
  Poor thing?

Oh, do you not know,
  That he's off long ago,
To a country where he'll find spring,
  Poor thing!

The north wind doth blow,
  And we shall have snow,
And what will the dormouse do then,
  Poor thing?

Rolled up like a ball,
　　In his nest snug and small.
He'll sleep till warm weather comes in,
　　Poor thing!

The north wind doth blow,
　　And we shall have snow,
And what will the honey-bee do then,
　　Poor thing?

In his hive he will stay,
　　Till the cold is away.
And then he'll come out in the spring,
　　Poor thing!

The north wind doth blow,
　　And we shall have snow,
And what will the children do then,
　　Poor things?

When lessons are done,
　　They must skip, jump and run,
Until they have made themselves warm,
　　Poor things!

THE BABES IN THE WOOD

My dear, do you know
How a long time ago,
Two poor little children,
Whose names I don't know,
Were stolen away,
On a fine summer's day,
And left in a wood,
As I've heard people say.

Among the trees high,
Beneath the blue sky,
They plucked the bright flowers
And watched the birds fly.
Then on blackberries fed
And strawberries red,
And when they were weary,
"We'll go home," they said.

But then it was night
And sad was their plight.
The sun it went down
And the moon gave no light.
They sobbed and they sighed,
And they bitterly cried,
And long before morning
They lay down and died.

And when they were dead,
The robins so red,
Brought strawberry leaves
And over them spread.
And all the day long,
The green branches among,
They'd prettily whistle
And this was their song—
"Poor babes in the wood,
Sweet babes in the wood,
Oh, the sad fate of
The babes in the wood."

MY PRETTY MAID MARY

My pretty maid Mary
She minds her dairy,
Whilst I go a-hoeing and a-mowing each morn.
    Merrily run the reel
    And the little spinning-wheel
While I am singing and mowing my corn.

MY BED

Four corners to my bed,
Four angels round my head,
One to watch and two to pray,
One to keep all fear away.

THERE WERE TWO BIRDS
SAT ON A STONE

There were two birds sat on a stone,
Fa, la, la, la, lal de;
Both flew away and then there was none,
Fa, la, la, la, lal de.
And so the poor stone
Was left all alone.
Fa, la, la, la, lal de.

THERE WAS A LITTLE GUINEA PIG

There was a little guinea pig,
Who, being little, was not big;
He always walked upon his feet
And never fasted when he ate.

When from a place he ran away,
He never at that place did stay;
And while he ran, as I am told,
He ne'er stood still for young or old.

He often squeaked and sometimes violent;
And when he squeaked he ne'er was silent;
Though ne'er instructed by a cat,
He knew a mouse was not a rat.

One day, as I am certified,
He took a whim and fairly died;
And, as I'm told by men of sense,
He never has been living since.

THREE JOLLY WELSHMEN

There were three jolly Welshmen,
  As I have heard men say,
And they would go a-hunting, boys,
  Upon St. David's Day.
And all the day they hunted
  But nothing could they find,
Except a ship a-sailing,
  A-sailing with the wind.

One said it surely was a ship,
  The second he said, "Nay."
The third declared it was a house
  With the chimney blown away.
Then all night they hunted
  And nothing could they find,
Except the moon a-gliding,
  A-gliding with the wind.

One said it surely was the moon,
  The second he said, "Nay."
The third declared it was a cheese
  With half of it cut away.
Then all next day they hunted
  And nothing could they find,
Except a hedgehog in a bush,
  And that they left behind.

One said it was a hedgehog,
　The second he said, "Nay."
The third, it was a pincushion,
　With pins stuck in wrong way.
Then all next day they hunted
　And nothing could they find,
Except a hare in a turnip field,
　And that they left behind.

One said it surely was a hare,
　The second he said, "Nay."
The third he said it was a calf,
　And the cow had run away.
Then all next day they hunted
　And nothing could they find,
But one owl in a holly tree,
　And that they left behind.

One said it surely was an owl,
　The second he said, "Nay."
The third said 'twas an aged man
　Whose beard was going grey.
Then all three jolly Welshmen
　Came riding home at last,
"For three days we have nothing killed,
　And never broke our fast!"

MY MOTHER SAID

My mother said, I never should,
Play with the gipsies in the wood.

If I did then she would say:
"Naughty girl to disobey!"

"Your hair shan't curl and
    your shoes shan't shine,
You gipsy girl you shan't be mine."

And my father said that if I did,
He'd rap my head with the tea-pot lid.

My mother said, I never should,
Play with the gipsies in the wood.

The wood was dark, the grass was green,
By came Sally with a tambourine.

I went to sea — no ship to get across,
I paid ten shillings for a blind white horse.

I upped on his back and
    was off in a crack.
"Sally, tell my mother I shall
    never come back!"

THE ROBIN AND THE WREN

The robin and the redbreast,
The robin and the wren,
If you take them out of their nest
You'll never thrive again.

The robin and the redbreast,
The martin and the swallow,
If you touch one of their eggs
Ill luck is sure to follow.

LITTLE DIAMONDS

A million little diamonds
Twinkled on the trees,
And all the little maidens said,
"A jewel, if you please!"

But while they held their hands outstretched,
To catch the diamonds gay,
A million little sunbeams came
And stole them all away!

HIGGLEDY, PIGGLEDY

Higgledy, piggledy, my black hen,
    She lays eggs for gentlemen.
      Gentlemen come every day
To see what my black hen doth lay.
Sometimes nine and sometimes ten,
    Higgledy, piggledy, my black hen.

PIGS!

Dearly loved children,
   Is it not a sin,
When you peel potatoes,
To throw away the skin?
   For the skin feeds pigs
   And pigs feed you.
Dearly loved children,
   Is this not true?

I HAD A LITTLE NUT TREE

I had a little nut tree,
Nothing would it bear,
But a silver nutmeg
And a golden pear.
The King of Spain's daughter
Came to visit me,
And all for the sake of my little nut tree!

I skipped over water,
I danced over sea,
And all the birds in the air,
Couldn't catch me!

I HAD A CAT

I had a cat and the cat pleased me,
I fed my cat by yonder tree:
Cat goes, "Mee-ow, mee-ow."

I had a hen and the hen pleased me,
I fed my hen by yonder tree:
Hen goes, "Cluck, cluck,"
Cat goes, "Mee-ow, mee-ow."

I had a duck and the duck pleased me,
I fed my duck by yonder tree:
Duck goes, "Quack, quack,"
Hen goes, "Cluck, cluck,"
Cat goes, "Mee-ow, mee-ow."

I had a sheep and the sheep pleased me,
I fed my sheep by yonder tree:
Sheep goes, "Baa, baa,"
Duck goes "Quack, quack"
Hen goes, "Cluck, cluck,"
Cat goes, "Mee-ow, mee-ow."

I had a pig and the pig pleased me,
I fed my pig by yonder tree:
Pig goes, "Grunt, grunt,"
Sheep goes, "Baa, baa,"
Duck goes, "Quack, quack,"
Hen goes, "Cluck, cluck,"
Cat goes, "Mee-ow, mee-ow."

I had a cow and the cow pleased me,
I fed my cow by yonder tree:
Cow goes, "Moo, moo,"
Pig goes, "Grunt, grunt,"
Sheep goes, "Baa, baa,"
Duck goes, "Quack, quack,"
Hen goes, "Cluck, cluck,"
Cat goes, "Mee-ow, mee-ow."

I had a horse and the horse pleased me,
I fed my horse by yonder tree:
Horse goes, "Neigh, neigh,"
Cow goes, "Moo, moo,"
Pig goes, "Grunt, grunt,"
Sheep goes, "Baa, baa,"
Duck goes, "Quack, quack,"
Hen goes, "Cluck, cluck,"
Cat goes, "Mee-ow, mee-ow."

I had a dog and the dog pleased me,
I fed my dog by yonder tree:
Dog goes, "Ruff, ruff,"
Horse goes, "Neigh, neigh,"
Cow goes, "Moo, moo,"
Pig goes, "Grunt, grunt,"
Sheep goes, "Baa, baa,"
Duck goes, "Quack, quack,"
Hen goes, "Cluck, cluck,"
Cat goes, "Mee-ow, mee-ow."

RING-A-RING OF ROSES

Ring-a-ring of roses,
A pocket full of posies.
Tishoo! Tishoo!
We all fall down.

RING-A-RING OF ROSES

THE QUEEN OF HEARTS

FEEL FREE TO DRESS UP!

Olivia's 7th B/DAY
party!

SUNDAY 23RD
NOVEMBER 2014

1300 - 1530 HRS

DROP OFF - SOMETHING
SPECIAL FLOWERS

PICK UP - THE WEE COFFEE
SHOP (OPPOSITE FLORIST)

ANNE-MARIE ON
FACEBOOK OR 07919341870
© Disney
BY 16TH NOVEMBER 2014

THE QUEEN OF HEARTS

The Queen of Hearts
She made some tarts,
All on a summer's day;
The Knave of Hearts
He stole the tarts,
And with them ran away.
The King of Hearts
Called for the tarts,
And beat the Knave full sore;
The Knave of Hearts
Brought back the tarts,
And said he'd ne'er steal more.

THE TWELVE DAYS OF CHRISTMAS

On the first day of Christmas
My true love sent to me:
A partridge in a pear tree.

On the second day of Christmas
My true love sent to me:
Two turtle doves,
And a partridge in a pear tree.

On the third day of Christmas
My true love sent to me:
Three French hens,
Two turtle doves,
And a partridge in a pear tree.

On the fourth day of Christmas,
My true love sent to me:
Four colly birds,
Three French hens,
Two turtle doves,
And a partridge in a pear tree.

On the fifth day of Christmas
My true love sent to me:
Five gold rings,

Four colly birds,
Three French hens,
Two turtle doves,
And a partridge in a pear tree.

On the sixth day of Christmas
My true love sent to me:
Six geese a-laying,
Five gold rings,
Four colly birds,
Three French hens,
Two turtle doves,
And a partridge in a pear tree.

On the seventh day of Christmas
My true love sent to me:
Seven swans a-swimming,
Six geese a-laying,
Five gold rings,
Four colly birds,
Three French hens,
Two turtle doves,
And a partridge in a pear tree.

On the eighth day of Christmas
My true love sent to me:
Eight maids a-milking,
Seven swans a-swimming,
Six geese a-laying,

continued on next page

Five gold rings,
Four colly birds,
Three French hens,
Two turtle doves,
And a partridge in a pear tree.

On the ninth day of Christmas
My true love sent to me:
Nine drummers drumming,
Eight maids a-milking,
Seven swans a-swimming,
Six geese a-laying,
Five gold rings,
Four colly birds,
Three French hens,
Two turtle doves,
And a partridge in a pear tree.

On the tenth day of Christmas
My true love sent to me:
Ten pipers piping,
Nine drummers drumming,
Eight maids a-milking,
Seven swans a-swimming,
Six geese a-laying,
Five gold rings,
Four colly birds,
Three French hens,
Two turtle doves,
And a partridge in a pear tree.

On the eleventh day of Christmas
My true love sent to me:
Eleven ladies dancing,
Ten pipers piping,
Nine drummers drumming,
Eight maids a-milking,
Seven swans a-swimming,
Six geese a-laying,
Five gold rings,
Four colly birds,
Three French hens,
Two turtle doves,
And a partridge in a pear tree.

On the twelfth day of Christmas
My true love sent to me:
Twelve lords a-leaping,
Eleven ladies dancing,
Ten pipers piping,
Nine drummers drumming,
Eight maids a-milking,
Seven swans a-swimming,
Six geese a-laying,
Five gold rings,
Four colly birds,
Three French hens,
Two turtle doves,
And a partridge in a pear tree.

THERE WAS AN OWL

There was an owl lived in an oak,
    Wisky, wasky, weedle;
And every word he ever spoke
    Was fiddle, faddle, feedle.

A soldier chanced to come that way,
    Wisky, wasky, weedle;
Says he, "I'll shoot you, silly bird,"
    Fiddle, faddle, feedle.

A MAN OF WORDS

A man of words and not of deeds
Is like a garden full of weeds;
For when the weeds begin to grow,
Then doth the garden overflow.

TO MARKET, TO MARKET, TO BUY A PLUM-CAKE

To market, to market, to buy a plum-cake;
Home again, home again, market is late.
To market, to market, to buy a plum-bun;
Home again, home again, market is done.

GREGORY GRIGGS

Gregory Griggs, Gregory Griggs,
Had twenty-seven different wigs.
He wore them up; he wore them down,
To please the people of the town;
He wore them east, he wore them west;
But he never could tell which he liked best.

HOGS IN THE GARDEN

Hogs in the garden, catch 'em, Towser;
    Cows in the cornfield, run, boys, run!
Cats in the cream-pot, run, girls! run, girls!
    Fire on the mountains, run, boys, run!

BLESS YOU, BLESS YOU, BUMBLE-BEE!

Bless you, bless you, bumble-bee!
Say, when will your wedding be?
If it be tomorrow day,
Take your wings and fly away.

I HAVE FOUR SISTERS

I have four sisters beyond the sea,
  Perry, merry, dixie, dominie.
And they each sent a present to me,
  Perry, merry, dixie, dominie.

The first sent a chicken without e'er a bone,
  Perry, merry, dixie, dominie.
The second a cherry without e'er a stone,
  Perry, merry, dixie, dominie.

The third sent a book which no man could read,
  Perry, merry, dixie, dominie.
The fourth sent a blanket, without e'er a thread,
  Perry, merry, dixie, dominie.

Can there be a chicken without e'er a bone?
  Perry, merry, dixie, dominie.
Can there be a cherry without any stone?
  Perry, merry, dixie, dominie.

Can there be a book which cannot be read?
Perry, merry, dixie, dominie.
Can there be a blanket without e'er a thread?
Perry, merry, dixie, dominie.

When the chicken's in the egg there is no bone,
Perry, merry, dixie, dominie.
When the cherry's in the bud there is no stone,
Perry, merry, dixie, dominie.

When the book's in the press it cannot be read,
Perry, merry, dixie, dominie.
When the blanket's in the fleece there is no thread,
Perry, merry, dixie, dominie.

NUTS AN' MAY

Here we come gathering nuts an' may,
  Nuts an' may, nuts an' may;
Here we come gathering nuts an' may,
  On a fine and frosty morning.

Who will you gather for nuts an' may,
  Nuts an' may, nuts an' may;
Who will you gather for nuts an' may,
  On a fine and frosty morning?

We'll gather Elsie for nuts an' may,
  Nuts an' may, nuts an' may;
We'll gather Elsie for nuts an' may,
  On a fine and frosty morning.

Who will you send to take her away,
  Take her away, take her away;
Who will you send to take her away,
  On a fine and frosty morning?

We will send Willie to take her away,
  Take her away, take her away;
We will send Willie to take her away,
  On a fine and frosty morning.

A CARRION CROW
SAT ON AN OAK

A carrion crow sat on an oak,
  Fol de riddle, lol de riddle, hi ding do,
Watching a tailor shape his coat.
  Sing heigh ho, the carrion crow,
  Fol de riddle, lol de riddle, hi ding do,

Wife, bring me my old bent bow,
  Fol de riddle, lol de riddle, hi ding do,
That I may shoot yon carrion crow.
  Sing heigh ho, the carrion crow,
  Fol de riddle, lol de riddle, hi ding do,

The tailor he shot and missed his mark,
  Fol de riddle, lol de riddle, hi ding do,
And shot his own sow right through the heart.
  Sing heigh ho, the carrion crow,
  Fol de riddle, lol de riddle, hi ding do,

Wife, bring brandy in a spoon,
  Fol de riddle, lol de riddle, hi ding do,
For the old sow is in a swoon.
  Sing heigh ho, the carrion crow,
  Fol de riddle, lol de riddle, hi ding do,

TRY AGAIN

'Tis a lesson you should heed,
    Try, try, try again;
If at first you don't succeed,
    Try, try, try again.

Once or twice though you should fail,
    Try again;
If at last you would prevail,
    Try again.
If we strive, 'tis no disgrace
Though we may not win the race;
What should you do in that case?
    Try again.

If you find your task is hard,
    Try again;
Time will bring you your reward,
    Try again.
All that other folks can do,
Why with patience should not you?
Only keep this rule in view—
    Try again.

LITTLE JENNY WREN

Little Jenny Wren
Fell sick upon a time;
In came Robin Redbreast,
And brought her cake and wine.

"Eat of my cake, Jenny,
Drink of my wine";
"Thank you, Robin, kindly,
You shall be mine."

Jenny she got well,
And stood upon her feet,
And told Robin plainly
She loved him not a bit.

Robin he was angry,
And hopped upon a twig,
Saying, "Out upon you! fie upon you!
Bold-faced jig."

LITTLE MAID, PRETTY MAID

"Little maid, pretty maid, whither goest thou?"
"Down in the forest to milk my cow."
"Shall I go with thee?" "No, not now;
When I send for thee, then come thou."

SHEPHERD'S CLOCKS

Shepherd's clocks don't tick or chime,
But they know to tell the time.

They can tell you, when you roam,
If it's time to think of home.

They can tell you—for they know—
If you must walk fast or slow.

They can tell if tea's begun:
If it is, you've got to *run*.

You must gather one—just so—
Hold it out, and blow, and blow;

If the feathers fly away
All at once, it's close of day.

(But be sure they fly together
With the one puff, *every* feather!)

If none flies, and all remain,
You had better try again:

Blow your cheeks out, tight as tight,
And give a puff with all your might.

Half may stay and half may go:
That means midday, you must know.

Blow again, and you will see
All will fly but two or three;

Then you know it's afternoon,
And tea-time must come on quite soon;

A gentle puff may leave just one;
Then you know play-time is done.

It is best to turn home then,
If you wish to play again

In the meadow with the flowers
Through the pleasant sunny hours

Tea-time is so quickly past,
Bed-time comes on, fast as fast;

Just a little sleep, and then
You are out of bed again;

You can see the sun, once more
Shining as he did before.

When all lessons are quite done,
Out you go, and off you run;

And shepherd's clocks tell, plain as plain,
That play-time has come round again.

Agnes Grozier Herbertson

LITTLE JACK HORNER

Little Jack Horner
Sat in a corner,
Eating a Christmas pie;
He put in his thumb,
And pulled out a plum,
And cried "What a good boy am I!"

LITTLE JACK HORNER

DING, DONG, BELL

DING, DONG, BELL

Ding, dong, bell,
Pussy's in the well.
    Who put her in?
    Little Tommy Green.
    Who pulled her out?
    Little Tommy Stout.
  What a naughty boy was that
  To hurt poor pussy cat,
Who never did him any harm,
But killed the mice in father's barn.

MERRY ARE THE BELLS

Merry are the bells, and merry would they ring,
Merry was myself, and merry could I sing.
With a merry ding-dong, happy, young and free,
And a merry sing-song, happy let us be!

Waddle goes your gait, and hollow are your hose,
Noddle goes your pate, and purple is your nose;
Merry is your sing-song, happy, young and free,
With a merry ding-dong, happy let us be!

Merry have we met, and merry have we been,
Merry let us part, and merry meet again:
With a merry sing-song, happy, young and free,
And a merry ding-dong, happy let us be!

DID YOU EVER?

Did you ever, ever, ever
   See a codfish who was clever?
Or a dolphin dance a hornpipe on his tail?
   Or a flounder play at skittles?
   Or a pig that left his victuals?
Or a porpoise sit and whistle on a rail?

      Or a double-breasted badger?
      Or a really starving cadger?
   Or a hermit who lives happily on roots –
      One who daily feeds and fattens?
      Or a pelican in pattens?
   Or an ostrich in knee breeches and top boots?

        Or a rosy-visaged baker?
        A white-hatted undertaker?
     Or a cap that wouldn't fit a dozen boys?
        Or a pea-green dromedary?
        Or a quiet cock canary?
     Or a cobbler who all his time employs?

          Or a jackdaw pass a spangle?
          Or an oyster turn a mangle?
        Or a cabman knocking gently at a door?
          If you've had your attention
          Drawn to half the things I mention,
        You've seen what never has been
          seen before.

THE OLD MAN WHO LIVED IN A WOOD

There was an old man who lived in a wood,
   As you may plainly see;
He said he could do as much work in a day
   As his wife could do in three.

"With all my heart," the old woman said;
   "If that you will allow,
Tomorrow you'll stay at home in my stead,
   And I'll go drive the plough.

"But you must milk the Tidy cow,
   For fear that she go dry;
And you must feed the little pigs
   That are within the sty;

"And you must mind the speckled hen,
   For fear she lay astray;
And you must reel the spool of yarn
   That I spun yesterday."

The old woman took a staff in her hand
   And went to drive the plough;

The old man took a pail in his hand,
  And went to milk the cow;

But Tidy hinched, and Tidy flinched,
  And Tidy broke his nose,
And Tidy gave him such a blow,
  That the blood ran down to his toes.

"Hi! Tidy! ho! Tidy! hi!
  Tidy, do stand still!
If ever I milk you, Tidy, again,
  'Twill be sore against my will."

He went to feed the little pigs
  That were within the sty;
He hit his head against the beam,
  And made the blood to fly.

He went to mind the speckled hen,
  For fear she'd lay astray,
And he forgot the spool of yarn
  His wife spun yesterday.

So he swore by the sun, the moon and stars,
  And the green leaves on the tree,
If his wife didn't do a day's work in her life,
  She should ne'er be ruled by he.

JOHNNY SHALL HAVE A NEW BONNET

Johnny shall have a new bonnet,
  And Johnny shall go to the fair,
And Johnny shall have a blue ribbon
  To tie up his bonny brown hair.

And why may not I love Johnny?
  And why may not Johnny love me?
And why may not I love Johnny,
  As well as another body?

And here's a leg for a stocking,
  And here's a leg for a shoe:
And he has a kiss for his daddy,
  And two for his mammy, I trow.

And why may not I love Johnny?
  And why may not Johnny love me?
And why may not I love Johnny,
  As well as another body?

"CROAK!" SAID THE TOAD

"Croak!" said the toad, "I'm hungry, I think;
To-day I've had nothing to eat or to drink.
I'll crawl to a garden and jump through the rails,
And there I'll sup finely on slugs and on snails."

"Ho, ho!" quoth the frog, "is that what you mean?
Then I'll hop away to the next muddy stream;
There I will drink, and eat worms and slugs too,
And then I shall have a snug supper like you."

BETTY PRINGLE

Betty Pringle had a little pig,
Not too little and not too big,
When he was alive he lived in clover,
But now he's dead, and that's all over.

So Billy Pringle he sat down and cried,

And Betty Pringle she laid down and died;

So there was the end of one, two and three:
    Billy Pringle, he,
    Betty Pringle, she,
    And the piggy wiggy wee.

THE MUFFIN MAN

Have you seen the muffin man?
  The muffin man, the muffin man.
Oh, have you seen the muffin man,
  Who lives down Drury Lane?

Oh yes, I've seen the muffin man,
  The muffin man, the muffin man.
Oh yes, I've seen the muffin man,
  Who lives down Drury Lane.

THERE WAS A CROOKED MAN

There was a crooked man,
And he walked a crooked mile,
And he found a crooked sixpence,
Beside a crooked stile.

He bought a crooked cat,
Which caught a crooked mouse,
And they all lived together
In a crooked little house.

HUSH LITTLE BABY

Hush little baby, don't say a word,
Papa's going to buy you a mocking bird.

If the mocking bird won't sing,
Papa's going to buy you a diamond ring.

If the diamond ring turns to brass,
Papa's going to buy you a looking glass.

If the looking glass gets broke,
Papa's going to buy you a billy-goat.

If that billy-goat runs away,
Papa's going to buy you another today.

MR. NOBODY

I know a funny little man,
As quiet as a mouse.
He does the mischief that is done,
In everybody's house!
Though no one ever sees his face,
Yet one and all agree,
That every plate we break was cracked
By Mr. Nobody.

'Tis he who always tears our books,
Who leaves the door ajar.
He picks the buttons from our shirts,
And scatters pins afar.
That squeaking door will always squeak
For prithee, don't you see?
We leave the oiling to be done
By Mr. Nobody.

He puts damp wood upon the fire,
So kettles will not boil.
His are the feet that bring in mud
And all the carpets soil.
The papers that are often lost –
Who had them last but he?
There's no one tosses them about
But Mr. Nobody.

The fingermarks upon the door
By none of us were made.
We never leave the blinds undone,
To let the curtains fade.
The ink we never spill! The boots,
That lying round you see,
Are not our boots – they all belong
To Mr. Nobody.

THE ANIMALS CAME IN TWO BY TWO

The animals came in two by two,
Hurrah, hurrah.
The centipede with the kangaroo,
Hurrah, hurrah.
And they all went into the ark
For to get out of the rain.

The animals came in three by three,
Hurrah, hurrah.
The elephant on the back of the flea,
Hurrah, hurrah.
And they all went into the ark
For to get out of the rain.

The animals came in four by four,
Hurrah, hurrah.
The camel, he got stuck in the door,
Hurrah, hurrah.
And they all went into the ark
For to get out of the rain.

The animals came in five by five,
Hurrah, hurrah.
The bees made sure to bring their hive,
Hurrah, hurrah.
And they all went into the ark
For to get out of the rain.

The animals came in six by six,
Hurrah, hurrah.
The monkey, he was up to his tricks,
Hurrah, hurrah.
And they all went into the ark
For to get out of the rain.

The animals went in seven by seven,
Hurrah, hurrah.
Some went to hell, and some to heaven,
Hurrah, hurrah.
And they all went into the ark
For to get out of the rain.

The animals went in eight by eight,
Hurrah, hurrah.
The worm was early, the bird was late,
Hurrah, hurrah.
And they all went into the ark
For to get out of the rain.

The animals went in nine by nine,
Hurrah, hurrah.
But the unicorn was not in time,
Hurrah, hurrah.
And they all went into the ark
For to get out of the rain.

AIKEN DRUM

There was a man lived in the moon,
   Lived in the moon, lived in the moon.
There was a man lived in the moon,
   And his name was Aiken Drum.

And he played upon a ladle,
   A ladle, a ladle.
And he played upon a ladle,
   And his name was Aiken Drum.

And his hat was made of good cream cheese,
   Good cream cheese, good cream cheese.
And his hat was made of good cream cheese,
   And his name was Aiken Drum.

And his coat was made of good roast beef,
   Good roast beef, good roast beef.
And his coat was made of good roast beef,
   And his name was Aiken Drum.

And his buttons were made of penny loaves,
   Penny loaves, penny loaves.
And his buttons were made of penny loaves,
   And his name was Aiken Drum.

And his waistcoat was made of a pastry crust,
    A pastry crust, a pastry crust.
And his waistcoat was made of a pastry crust,
    And his name was Aiken Drum.

There was a man lived in the moon,
    Lived in the moon, lived in the moon.
There was a man lived in the moon,
    And his name was Aiken Drum.

LITTLE BOY BLUE

Little Boy Blue, come blow your horn!
The sheep's in the meadow, the cow's in the corn.
Where's the boy that looks after the sheep?
He's under the haycock, fast asleep.
Will you wake him? No, not I;
For if I do, he'll be sure to cry.

LITTLE BOY BLUE

PEASE PUDDING HOT

PEASE PUDDING HOT

Pease pudding hot,
  Pease pudding cold,
Pease pudding in the pot,
  Nine days old.

Some like it hot,
  Some like it cold,
Some like it in the pot,
  Nine days old.

MY FATHER HE DIED

My father he died, but I can't tell you how,
He left me six horses to drive in my plough:
  With my wing wang waddle oh,
  Jack sing saddle oh,
  Blowsey boys bubble oh,
  Under the broom.

I sold my six horses, and I bought me a cow,
I'd fain have made a fortune, but did not know how:
  With my wing wang waddle oh,
  Jack sing saddle oh,
  Blowsey boys bubble oh,
  Under the broom.

I sold my cow, and I bought me a calf;
I'd fain have made a fortune, but lost the best half:
  With my wing wang waddle oh,
  Jack sing saddle oh,
  Blowsey boys bubble oh,
  Under the broom.

I sold my calf, and I bought me a cat;
A pretty thing she was, in my chimney corner sat:
    With my wing wang waddle oh,
    Jack sing saddle oh,
    Blowsey boys bubble oh,
    Under the broom.

I sold my cat, and bought me a mouse;
He carried fire in his tail, and burnt down my house:
    With my wing wang waddle oh,
    Jack sing saddle oh,
    Blowsey boys bubble oh,
    Under the broom.

PUSSY

I like little pussy, her coat is so warm;
And if I don't hurt her, she'll do me no harm.
So I'll not pull her tail, nor drive her away,
But pussy and I very gently will play.
She shall sit by my side, and I'll give her some food;
And she'll love me because I am gentle and good.

I'll pat pretty pussy, and then she will purr;
And thus show her thanks for my kindness to her.
But I'll not pinch her ears, nor tread on her paw,
Lest I should provoke her to use her sharp claw.
I never will vex her, nor make her displeased—
For pussy don't like to be worried and teased.

I HAD A LITTLE HOBBY-HORSE

I had a little hobby-horse,
  And it was dapple grey.
Its head was made of pea-straw;
  Its tail was made of hay.

I sold it to an old woman
  For a copper groat;
And I'll not sing my song again
  Without a new coat.

THE RAINBOW AND THE CUCKOO

Which is the bow that has no arrow?
The rainbow, that never killed a sparrow.
Which is the singer that hath but one song?
The cuckoo, who singeth it all day long.

HINK, MINX!

Hink, minx! the old witch winks,
The fat begins to fry.
There's nobody at home but jumping Joan,
Father, mother and I.

NONSENSES

There was an Old Man with a beard,
Who said, "It is just as I feared! –
    Two owls and a hen,
    Four larks and a wren,
Have all built their nests in my beard!"

There was an Old Lady of Chertsey,
Who made a remarkable curtsey;
    She twirled round and round,
    Till she sank underground,
Which distressed all the people of Chertsey.

There was an Old Man in a tree,
Who was horribly bored by a bee;
    When they said, "Does it buzz?"
    He replied, "Yes, it does!
It's a regular brute of a bee!"

There was an Old Man who said, "How
Shall I flee from this horrible cow?
  I will sit on this stile,
  And continue to smile,
Which may soften the heart of that cow."

There was an Old Man who said, "Hush!
I perceive a young bird in this bush!"
  When they said, "Is it small?"
  He replied, "Not at all!
It is four times as big as the bush!"

There was an Old Person of Gretna,
Who rushed down the crater of Etna;
  When they said, "Is it hot?"
  He replied, "No, it's not!"
That mendacious Old Person of Gretna.

There was an Old Man of Dumbree,
Who taught little owls to drink tea;
  For he said, "To eat mice,
  Is not proper or nice,"
That amiable Man of Dumbree.

Edward Lear

189

THE CUCKOO

In April
Come he will.
In May
He sings all day.
In June
He's out of tune.
In July
He prepares to fly.
In August
Go he must.

CROSS PATCH

Cross Patch, draw the latch,
　Sit by the fire and spin;
Take a cup, and drink it up,
　Then call your neighbours in.

FIDDLE-DE-DEE

Fiddle-de-dee, fiddle-de-dee,
The fly shall marry the humble-bee.
They went to church, and married was she:
The fly has married the humble-bee.

ANDREW, THE SCHOLAR

As I was going o'er Westminster Bridge,
I met with a Westminster scholar;
He pulled off his cap *an' drew* off his glove,
And wished me a very good morrow.
Pray what was the name of that scholar?

LADY-BIRD

Lady-bird! Lady-bird! fly away home;
 The field mouse is gone to her nest,
The daisies have shut up their sleepy red eyes,
 And the bees and the birds are at rest.

Lady-bird! Lady-bird! fly away home;
 The glow-worm is lighting her lamp,
The dew's falling fast, and your fine speckled wings
 Will flag with the close-clinging damp.

Lady-bird! Lady-bird! fly away home;
 The fairy bells tinkle afar;
Make haste, or they'll catch you and harness you fast
 With a cobweb to Oberon's car.

LITTLE ROBIN REDBREAST

Little Robin Redbreast sat upon a tree:
Up went pussy-cat, and down went he;
Down came pussy-cat, and away Robin ran;
Says little Robin Redbreast, "Catch me if you can."

Little Robin Redbreast hopped upon a wall;
Pussy-cat jumped after him, and almost got a fall.
Little Robin chirped and sung, and what did Pussy
    say?
Pussy-cat said "Mew," and Robin flew away.

OF ALL THE BRAVE BIRDS

Of all the brave birds that e'er I did see,
The owl is the fairest by far to me;
For all the day long she sits on a tree,
And when the night comes away flies she.
            Tu-whit, tu-whoo,
            Sir knave to you,
Her song is well sung, Tu-whit, tu-whoo.

LITTLE JUMPING JOAN

Here I am,
Little jumping Joan;
When nobody's with me
I'm always alone.

A LITTLE COCK SPARROW

A little cock sparrow sat on a tree,
Looking as happy as happy could be,
Till a boy came by with his bow and arrow:
Says he, "I will shoot the little cock sparrow.

"His body will make me a nice little stew,
And perhaps there'll be some for a little pie too."
Says the little cock sparrow, "I'll be shot if I stay."
So he flapped his wings and flew away.

OH, THAT I WAS WHERE I WOULD BE!

Oh, that I was where I would be,
Then would I be where I am not!
But where I am I must be,
And where I would be I cannot.

HUMPTY DUMPTY'S SONG

In winter, when the fields are white,
I sing this song for your delight.

In spring, when woods are getting green,
I'll try and tell you what I mean.

In summer, when the days are long,
Perhaps you'll understand the song.

In autumn, when the leaves are brown,
Take pen and ink, and write it down.

I sent a message to the fish:
I told them "This is what I wish."

The little fishes of the sea,
They sent an answer back to me.

The little fishes" answer was
"We cannot do it, Sir, because –"

I sent to them again to say
"It will be better to obey."

The fishes answered, with a grin,
"Why, what a temper you are in!"

I told them once, I told them twice:
They would not listen to advice.

I took a kettle large and new,
Fit for the deed I had to do.

My heart went hop, my heart went thump:
I filled the kettle at the pump.

Then someone came to me and said
"The little fishes are in bed."

I said to him, I said it plain,
"Then you must wake them up again."

I said it very loud and clear:
I went and shouted in his ear.

But he was very stiff and proud:
He said "You needn't shout so loud!"

And he was very proud and stiff:
He said "I'd go and wake them, if –"

I took a corkscrew from the shelf:
I went to wake them up myself.

And when I found the door was locked,
I pulled and pushed and kicked and knocked.

And when I found the door was shut,
I tried to turn the handle, but –

Lewis Carroll

DAME, WHAT MAKES YOUR DUCKS TO DIE?

Dame, what makes your ducks to die?
What ails 'em? what ails 'em?
They kick up their heels and there they lie:
What ails 'em now?
Heigh, ho! heigh, ho!

Dame, what makes your ducks to die?
What ails 'em? what ails 'em?
Heigh, ho! heigh, ho!
Dame, what ails your ducks to die?
Eating o' polly-wigs, eating o' polly-wigs,
Heigh, ho! heigh, ho!

THE GIRL IN THE LANE

The girl in the lane,
That couldn't speak plain,
Cried, gobble, gobble, gobble.
The man on the hill,
That couldn't stand still,
Went hobble, hobble, hobble.

HANNAH BANTRY

Hannah Bantry in the pantry,
   Eating a mutton bone;
How she gnawed it, how she clawed it,
   When she found she was alone!

GREY GOOSE AND GANDER

Grey goose and gander,
   Waft your wings together,
And carry the good king's daughter
   Over the river.

THE DOVE SAYS COO, COO

The dove says coo, coo, what shall I do?
I can scarce maintain two.
Pooh, pooh, says the wren, I have got ten,
And keep them all like gentlemen!

JACK SPRAT

Jack Sprat could eat no fat,
His wife could eat no lean;
And so between them both, you see,
They licked the platter clean.

JACK SPRAT

OLD MOTHER HUBBARD

OLD MOTHER HUBBARD

Old Mother Hubbard she went to the cupboard
To get her poor dog a bone,
But when she got there the cupboard was bare,
And so the poor dog had none.

She went to the baker's
To buy him some bread;
But when she came back
The poor dog was dead.

She went to the joiner's
To buy him a coffin;
But when she came back
The poor dog was laughing.

She took a clean dish
To get him some tripe;
But when she came back
He was smoking a pipe.

She went to the fishmonger's
To buy him some fish;
And when she came back
He was licking the dish.

continued on next page

She went to the tavern
For white wine and red;
But when she came back
The dog stood on his head.

She went to the hatter's
To buy him a hat;
But when she came back
He was feeding the cat.

She went to the barber's
To buy him a wig;
But when she came back
He was dancing a jig.

She went to the cobbler's
To buy him some shoes;
But when she came back
He was reading the news.

She went to the tailor's
To buy him a coat;
But when she came back
He was riding a goat.

She went to the fruiterer's
To buy him some fruit;
But when she came back
He was playing the flute.

She went to the seamstress
To buy him some linen;
But when she came back
The dog was spinning.

The dame made a curtsey,
The dog made a bow;
The dame said, "Your servant,"
The dog said, "Bow, wow!"

AS I WAS GOING UP THE HILL

As I was going up the hill,
   I met with Jack the piper;
And all the tune that he could play
   Was, "Tie up your petticoats tighter."

I tied them once, I tied them twice,
   I tied them three times over;
And all the song that he could sing
   Was, "Carry me safe to Dover."

TOMMY SNOOKS AND BESSY BROOKS

As Tommy Snooks and Bessy Brooks
   Were walking out one Sunday,
Says Tommy Snooks to Bessy Brooks,
   "Tomorrow will be Monday."

A APPLE PIE

A apple pie;
  B bit it;
    C cut it;
      D dealt it;
        E eat (ate) it;
          F fought for it;
            G got it;
              H had it;
                I inked it;
                  J joined it;
                    K kept it;
                      L longed for it;
                        M mourned for it;
                          N nodded at it;
                            O opened it;
                              P peeped in it;
                                Q quartered it;
                                  R ran for it;
                                    S stole it;
                                      T took it;
                                        V viewed it;
                                          W wanted it;
                                            X Y, Z and ampersand*
                                            All wished for a piece in hand.

* Ampersand *is* and.

THE OWL AND THE PUSSY-CAT

The Owl and the Pussy-cat went to sea
   In a beautiful pea-green boat,
They took some honey, and plenty of money,
   Wrapped up in a five-pound note.
The Owl looked up to the stars above,
   And sang to a small guitar,
"O lovely Pussy! O Pussy, my love,
   What a beautiful Pussy you are,
      You are,
      You are!
What a beautiful Pussy you are!"

Pussy said to the Owl, "You elegant fowl!
   How charmingly sweet you sing!
O let us be married! too long we have tarried:
   But what shall we do for a ring?"
They sailed away, for a year and a day,
   To the land where the Bong-tree grows,
And there in a wood a Piggy-wig stood
   With a ring at the end of his nose,
      His nose,
      His nose,
With a ring at the end of his nose.

"Dear Pig, are you willing to sell for one shilling
    Your ring?" Said the Piggy, "I will."
So they took it away, and were married next day
    By the Turkey who lives on the hill.
They dined on mince, and slices of quince,
    Which they ate with a runcible spoon;
And hand in hand, on the edge of the sand,
    They danced by the light of the moon,
        The moon,
        The moon,
They danced by the light of the moon.

Edward Lear

O SOLDIER, SOLDIER

"O soldier, soldier, will you marry me,
    With your musket, fife and drum?"
"Oh no, sweet maid, I cannot marry you,
    For I have no coat to put on."

So off she went to the tailor's shop,
    As fast as legs could run,
And bought him a coat of the very, very best,
    And the soldier put it on.

"O soldier, soldier, will you marry me,
    With your musket, fife and drum?"
"Oh no, sweet maid, I cannot marry you,
    For I have no shoes to put on."

So off she went to the cobbler's shop,
    As fast as legs could run,
And bought a pair of the very, very best,
    And the soldier put them on.

"O soldier, soldier, will you marry me,
    With your musket, fife and drum?"
"Oh no, sweet maid, I cannot marry you,
    For I have no socks to put on."

So off she went to the sock-maker's shop,
    As fast as legs could run,
And bought him a pair of the very, very best,
    And the soldier put them on.

"O soldier, soldier, will you marry me,
    With your musket, fife and drum?"
"Oh no, sweet maid, I cannot marry you,
    For I have no hat to put on."

So off she went to the hatter's shop,
    As fast as legs could run,
And bought him a hat of the very, very best,
    And the soldier put it on.

"O soldier, soldier, will you marry me,
    With your musket, fife and drum?"
"Oh no, sweet maid, I cannot marry you,
    For I have a wife at home!"

WOE IS ME!

Woe is me, woe is me!
The acorn's not yet
Fallen from the tree,
That's to grow the wood,
That's to make the cradle,
That's to rock the bairn,
That'll grow to the man,
Who's to marry me!

IT'S RAINING

It's raining, it's pouring,
    The old man's snoring.
He went to bed,
    And bumped his head,
And couldn't get up
    In the morning.

BETTY BOTTER

Betty Botter bought some butter,
   "But," she said, "the butter's bitter!
If I put it in my batter,
   It will make my batter bitter.
But a bit of better butter
   Will make my batter better!"

So she bought a bit of butter,
   Better than the bitter butter.
And she put it in her batter,
   And the batter was not bitter.
So 'twas better Betty Botter
   Bought some better butter.

ONE DAY I SAW

One day I saw a big brown cow
  Raise her head and chew.
I said, "Good morning, Mrs. Cow,"
  But all she said was, "Moo!"

One day I saw a woolly lamb,
  I followed it quite far.
I said, "Good morning, little lamb,"
  But all it said was, "Baa!"

One day I saw a dappled horse,
  Cropping in the hay.
I said, "Good morning, Mr. Horse,"
  But all he said was, "Neigh!"

One day I saw a tabby cat,
  Walking through the dew.
I said, "Good morning, tabby cat,"
  But all she said was, "Mew!"

One day I saw a pretty bird,
  Which fluttered at my feet.
I said, "Good morning, little bird,"
  But all he said was, "Tweet!"

One day I saw a greedy pig,
  With mud all down his front.
I said, "Good morning, Mr. Pig,"
  But all he said was, "Grunt!"

One day I saw a friendly duck,
  With feathers on her back.
I said, "Good morning, Mrs. Duck,"
  But all she said was, "Quack!"

One day I saw a field mouse
  And thought that he would speak.
I said, "Good morning, tiny mouse,"
  But all he said was, "Squeak!"

FERRY ME ACROSS THE WATER

"Ferry me across the water,
  Do, boatman, do,"
"If you've a penny in your purse
  I'll ferry you."

"I have a penny in my purse,
  And my eyes are blue;
So ferry me across the water,
  Do, boatman, do."

"Step into my ferry-boat,
  Be they black or blue,
And for the penny in your purse
  I'll ferry you."

Christina Rossetti

ONE, TWO

One, two,
Buckle your shoe.

Three, four,
Knock at the door.

Five, six,
Pick up sticks.

Seven, eight,
Lay them straight.

Nine, ten,
A big fat hen.

Eleven, twelve,
Dig and delve.

Thirteen, fourteen,
Maids a-courting.

Fifteen, sixteen,
Maids in the kitchen.

Seventeen, eighteen,
Maids in waiting.

Nineteen, twenty,
My plate's empty.

MARY, MARY, QUITE CONTRARY

Mary, Mary, quite contrary,
    How does your garden grow?
With cockle shells and silver bells
    And cowslips all in a row.

RUB A DUB DUB

Rub a dub dub,
Three men in a tub;
And who do you think they be?
The butcher, the baker,
The candlestick-maker;
Turn 'em out, knaves all three!

THIS LITTLE PIG WENT TO MARKET

This little pig went to market;
This little pig stayed at home;
This little pig had roast beef;
This little pig had none;
This little pig cried *"Wee, wee, wee!"*
    All the way home.

MARY, MARY, QUITE CONTRARY

RUB A DUB DUB

THIS LITTLE PIG WENT TO MARKET

SIMPLE SIMON

SIMPLE SIMON

Simple Simon met a pieman
Going to the fair;
Says Simple Simon to the pieman,
"Let me taste your ware."

Says the pieman to Simple Simon,
"Show me first your penny."
Says Simple Simon to the pieman,
"Indeed I have not any."

Simple Simon went a-fishing,
For to catch a whale;
All the water he had got
Was in his mother's pail.

He went to take a bird's nest,
Was built upon a bough;
The branch gave way, and Simon fell
Into a dirty slough.

He went to shoot a wild duck,
But wild duck flew away;
Says Simon, "I can't hit him,
Because he will not stay."

continued on next page

He went to catch a dickey-bird,
And thought he could not fail,
Because he'd got a little salt
To put upon his tail.

Simple Simon went a-hunting,
For to catch a hare;
He rode an ass about the streets,
But couldn't find one there.

He went for to eat honey,
Out of the mustard pot;
He bit his tongue until he cried,
That was all the good he got.

He went to ride a spotted cow,
That had a little calf;
She threw him down upon the ground,
Which made the people laugh.

Once Simon made a great snowball,
And brought it in to roast;
He laid it down before the fire,
And soon the ball was lost.

He went to slide upon the ice,
Before the ice would bear;
Then he plunged in above his knees,
Which made poor Simon stare.

Simple Simon went to look
If plums grew on a thistle;
He pricked his fingers very much,
Which made poor Simon whistle.

He went for water in a sieve,
But soon it all ran through.
And now poor Simple Simon
Bids you all adieu.

TWO LITTLE KITTENS

Two little kittens, one stormy night,
Began to quarrel, and then to fight;
One had a mouse, the other had none,
And that's the way the quarrel begun.

"I'll have that mouse," said the biggest cat;
"You'll have that mouse? We'll see about that!"
"I *will* have that mouse," said the eldest son;
"You *shan't* have the mouse," said the little one.

I told you before 'twas a stormy night
When these two little kittens began to fight;
The old woman seized her sweeping broom,
And swept the two kittens right out of the room.

The ground was covered with frost and snow,
And the two little kittens had nowhere to go;
So they laid them down on the mat at the door,
While the old woman finished sweeping the floor.

Then they crept in, as quiet as mice,
All wet with the snow, and as cold as ice,
For they found it was better, that stormy night,
To lie down and sleep than to quarrel and fight.

IF WISHES WERE HORSES

If wishes were horses,
    Beggars would ride;
If turnips were watches,
    I'd wear one by my side.

A DILLER, A DOLLAR

A diller, a dollar,
    A ten o'clock scholar,
What makes you come so soon?
    You used to come at ten o'clock,
But now you come at noon.

ONE, TWO, THREE, FOUR

One, two, three, four,
Mary at the cottage door;
Five, six, seven, eight,
Eating cherries off a plate.
O-U-T spells out!

ROBIN HOOD

Robin Hood, Robin Hood,
Is in the mickle wood!
Little John, Little John,
He to the town is gone.

Little John, Little John,
  If he comes no more,
Robin Hood, Robin Hood,
  He will fret full sore!

HUSH BABY, MY DOLL

Hush baby, my doll, I pray you don't cry,
And I'll give you some bread and milk by and by;
Or perhaps you like custard, or maybe a tart,
Then to either you're welcome with all of my heart.

THE TWENTY-NINTH OF MAY

The twenty-ninth of May
  Is oak-apple day;
If you don't give us a holiday
  We'll all run away.

A RED SKY IN THE MORNING

A red sky in the morning
Is the shepherd's warning;
A red sky at night
Is the shepherd's delight.

WHAT DO I SEE?

What do I see?
  A bumble-bee
Sit on a rose
  And wink at me!

What do you mean
  By *hum, hum, hum?*
If you mean me,
  I dare not come!

BESSY BELL AND MARY GRAY

Bessy Bell and Mary Gray,
  They were two bonnie lasses:
They built their house upon the lea,
  And covered it with rushes.

Bessy kept the garden gate,
  And Mary kept the pantry;
Bessy always had to wait,
  While Mary lived in plenty.

THREE CHILDREN SLIDING ON THE ICE

Three children sliding on the ice,
  Upon a summer's day;
It so fell out, they all fell in,
  The rest they ran away.

Now had these children been at home,
  Or sliding on dry ground,
Ten thousand pounds to one penny
  They had not all been drowned.

You parents that have children dear,
  And eke you that have done,
If you would have them safe abroad,
  Pray keep them safe at home.

DAFFY-DOWN-DILLY

Daffy-down-dilly has come up to town,
  In a yellow petticoat and a green gown.

ELIZABETH, ELSPETH, BETSY AND BESS

Elizabeth, Elspeth, Betsy and Bess,
They all went together to seek a bird's nest.
They found a bird's nest with five feathers in,
They all took one, and left four in.

I HAD A LITTLE HUSBAND

I had a little husband,
    No bigger than my thumb;
I put him in a pint pot,
    And there I bid him drum.

I bought a little horse,
    That galloped up and down;
I bridled him, and saddled him
    And sent him out of town.

I gave him some garters
    To garter up his hose,
And a little handkerchief
    To wipe his pretty nose.

THE JUMBLIES

They went to sea in a Sieve, they did,
   In a Sieve they went to sea:
In spite of all their friends could say,
On a winter's morn, on a stormy day,
   In a Sieve they went to sea!
And when the Sieve turned round and round,
And everyone cried, "You'll all be drowned!"
They called aloud, "Our Sieve ain't big,
But we don't care a button! we don't care a fig!
   In a Sieve we'll go to sea!"
     Far and few, far and few,
       Are the lands where the Jumblies live;
       Their heads are green, and their hands are blue,
       And they went to sea in a Sieve.

They sailed away in a Sieve, they did,
   In a Sieve they sailed so fast,
With only a beautiful pea-green veil
Tied with a riband by way of a sail,
   To a small tobacco-pipe mast;
And everyone said, who saw them go,
"O won't they be soon upset, you know!
For the sky is dark, and the voyage is long,
And happen what may, it's extremely wrong
   In a Sieve to sail so fast!"
     Far and few, far and few,
       Are the lands where the Jumblies live;
       Their heads are green, and their hands are blue,
       And they went to sea in a Sieve.

The water it soon came in, it did,
    The water it soon came in;
So to keep them dry, they wrapped their feet
In a pinky paper all folded neat,
    And they fastened it down with a pin.
And they passed the night in a crockery-jar,
And each of them said, "How wise we are!
Though the sky be dark, and the voyage be long,
Yet we never can think we were rash or wrong,
    While round in our Sieve we spin!"
        Far and few, far and few,
            Are the lands where the Jumblies live;
        Their heads are green, and their hands are blue,
            And they went to sea in a Sieve.

And all night long they sailed away;
    And when the sun went down,
They whistled and warbled a moony song
To the echoing sound of a coppery gong,
    In the shade of the mountains brown.
"O Timballoo! How happy we are,
When we live in a sieve and a crockery-jar,
And all night long in the moonlight pale,
We sail away with a pea-green sail,
    In the shade of the mountains brown!"
        Far and few, far and few,
            Are the lands where the Jumblies live;
        Their heads are green, and their hands are blue,
            And they went to sea in a Sieve.

continued on next page

They sailed to the Western Sea, they did,
    To a land all covered with trees,
And they bought an Owl, and a useful Cart,
And a pound of Rice, and a Cranberry Tart,
    And a hive of silvery Bees.
And they bought a Pig, and some green Jackdaws,
And a lovely Monkey with lollipop paws,
And forty bottles of Ring-Bo-Ree,
    And no end of Stilton Cheese.
        Far and few, far and few,
            Are the lands where the Jumblies live;
        Their heads are green, and their hands are blue,
            And they went to sea in a Sieve.

And in twenty years they all came back,
    In twenty years or more,
And everyone said, "How tall they've grown!
For they've been to the Lakes, and the Terrible Zone,
    And the hills of the Chankly Bore;
And they drank their health, and gave them a feast
Of dumplings made of beautiful yeast;
And everyone said, "If we only live,
We too will go to sea in a Sieve,
    To the hills of the Chankly Bore!"
        Far and few, far and few,
            Are the lands where the Jumblies live;
        Their heads are green, and their hands are blue,
            And they went to sea in a Sieve.

Edward Lear

DON'T-CARE

Don't-care didn't care,
Don't-care was wild.
Don't-care stole plum and pear
Like any beggar's child.

Don't-care was made to care,
Don't-care was hung.
Don't-care was put in a pot
And boiled till he was done.

WHEN THE WIND BLOWS

When the wind blows,
Then the mill goes;
When the wind drops,
Then the mill stops.

ONE TO MAKE READY

One to make ready,
And two to prepare;
Good Luck to the rider,
And away goes the mare.

THERE WAS A MONKEY

There was a monkey climbed up a tree;
When he fell down, then down fell he.

There was a crow sat on a stone;
When he was gone, then there was none.

There was an old wife did eat an apple;
When she had ate two, she had ate a couple.

There was a horse going to the mill;
When he went on, he stood not still.

There was a butcher cut his thumb;
When it did bleed, then blood did come.

There was a lackey ran a race;
When he ran fast, he ran apace.

There was a cobbler clouting shoon;
When they were mended, they were done.

There was a chandler making candle;
When he them strip, he did them handle.

There was a navy went into Spain;
When it returned it came again.

TRUTH THE BEST

Yesterday Rebecca Mason,
  In the parlour by herself,
Broke a handsome china basin,
  Placed upon the mantelshelf.

Quite alarmed, she thought of going
  Very quietly away,
Not a single person knowing
  Of her being there that day.

But Rebecca recollected
  She was taught deceit to shun;
And the moment she reflected,
  Told her mother what was done;

Who commended her behaviour,
Loved her better, and forgave her.

THE MONTHS

Thirty days hath September,
April, June and November.
All the rest have thirty-one,
Excepting February alone,
And that has twenty-eight days clear,
And twenty-nine in each leap year.

OLD KING COLE

Old King Cole was a merry old soul,
And a merry old soul was he;
He called for his pipe, he called for his glass,
And he called for his fiddlers three.

Every fiddler he had a fine fiddle,
And a very fine fiddle had he;
Twee-tweedle-dee, tweedle-dee, went the fiddlers.
Oh, there's none so rare as can compare
With King Cole and his fiddlers three!

OLD KING COLE

LUCY LOCKET LOST HER POCKET

LUCY LOCKET LOST HER POCKET

Lucy Locket lost her pocket;
Kitty Fisher found it;
There was not a penny in it,
But a ribbon round it.

THE FARMER'S IN HIS DEN

The farmer's in his den,
  The farmer's in his den,
E-I-E-I,
  The farmer's in his den.

The farmer wants a wife,
  The farmer wants a wife,
E-I-E-I,
  The farmer wants a wife.

The wife wants a child,
  The wife wants a child,
E-I-E-I,
  The wife wants a child.

The child wants a nurse,
  The child wants a nurse,
E-I-E-I,
  The child wants a nurse.

The nurse wants a dog,
  The nurse wants a dog,
E-I-E-I,
  The nurse wants a dog.

We all pat the dog,
  We all pat the dog,
E-I-E-I,
  We all pat the dog.

A DOG AND A COCK

A dog and a cock a journey once took,
They travelled along till 'twas late;
   The dog he made free
   In the hollow of a tree,
And the cock on the boughs of it sate.

   The cock, nothing knowing,
   In the morn fell a-crowing,
Upon which comes a fox to the tree;
   Says he, "I declare
   Your voice is above
All the creatures I ever did see.

   "Oh, would you come down,
   I would hug you, my own!"
Said the cock, "There's a porter beneath;
   If you'll ask his advice,
   I'll come down in a trice!"
So the fox did, and was chased 'cross the heath!

THE WALRUS AND THE CARPENTER

The sun was shining on the sea,
   Shining with all his might:
He did his very best to make
   The billows smooth and bright –
And this was odd, because it was
   The middle of the night.

The moon was shining sulkily,
   Because she thought the sun
Had got no business to be there
   After the day was done –
"It's very rude of him," she said,
   "To come and spoil the fun!"

The sea was wet as wet could be,
   The sands were dry as dry.
You could not see a cloud, because
   No cloud was in the sky:
No birds were flying overhead –
   There were no birds to fly.

The Walrus and the Carpenter
    Were walking close at hand;
They wept like anything to see
    Such quantities of sand:
"If this were only cleared away,"
    They said, "it *would* be grand!"

"If seven maids with seven mops
    Swept it for half a year,
Do you suppose," the Walrus said,
    "That they could get it clear?"
"I doubt it," said the Carpenter,
    And shed a bitter tear.

"O Oysters come and walk with us!"
    The Walrus did beseech.
"A pleasant walk, a pleasant talk,
    Along the briny beach:
We cannot do with more than four,
    To give a hand to each."

The eldest Oyster looked at him,
    But never a word he said:
The eldest Oyster winked his eye,
    And shook his heavy head—
Meaning to say he did not choose
    To leave the oyster-bed.

continued on next page

But four young Oysters hurried up,
    All eager for the treat:
Their coats were brushed, their faces washed,
    Their shoes were clean and neat –
And this was odd, because, you know,
    They hadn't any feet.

Four others Oysters followed them,
    And yet another four;
And thick and fast they came at last,
    And more, and more, and more –
All hopping through the frothy waves,
    And scrambling to the shore.

The Walrus and the Carpenter
    Walked on a mile or so,
And then they rested on a rock
    Conveniently low:
And all the little Oysters stood
    And waited in a row.

"The time has come," the Walrus said,
    "To talk of many things:
Of shoes – and ships – and sealing-wax –
    Of cabbages – and kings –
And why the sea is boiling hot –
    And whether pigs have wings."

"But wait a bit," the Oysters cried,
    "Before we have our chat;
For some of us are out of breath,
    And all of us are fat!"
"No hurry!" said the Carpenter.
    They thanked him much for that.

"A loaf of bread," the Walrus said,
    "Is what we chiefly need:
Pepper and vinegar besides
    Are very good indeed–
Now if you're ready, Oysters dear,
    We can begin to feed."

"But not on us!" the Oysters cried,
    Turning a little blue.
"After such kindness, that would be
    A dismal thing to do!"
"The night is fine," the Walrus said,
    "Do you admire the view?"

Lewis Carroll

CRY, BABY, CRY

Cry, baby, cry,
   Put your finger in your eye;
Then go and tell your mother it was not I.

RAIN, RAIN, GO AWAY

Rain, rain, go away,
   Come again another day;
Little Johnny wants to play.

HOW MANY MILES?

How many miles to Babylon?
Threescore miles and ten.

Can I get there by candlelight?
Yes, and back again.

If your heels are nimble and light,
You will get there by candlelight.

THE SHEEP

"Lazy sheep, pray tell me why
In the pleasant fields you lie,
Eating grass, and daisies white,
From the morning till the night?
Everything can something do,
But what kind of use are you?"

"Nay, my little master, nay,
Do not serve me so, I pray;
Don't you see the wool that grows
On my back, to make you clothes?
Cold, and very cold, you'd be
If you had not wool from me.

"True, it seems a pleasant thing,
To nip the daisies in the spring;
But many chilly nights I pass
On the cold and dewy grass,
Or pick a scanty dinner, where
All the common's brown and bare.

"Then the farmer comes at last,
When the merry spring is past,
And cuts my woolly coat away,
To warm you in the winter's day:
Little master, this is why
In the pleasant fields I lie."

Ann and Jane Taylor

WHERE DID YOU COME FROM, BABY DEAR?

Where did you come from, baby dear?
Out of the everywhere into here.

Where did you get your eyes so blue?
Out of the sky as I came through.

What makes the light in them sparkle and spin?
Some of the starry spikes left in.

Where did you get that little tear?
I found it waiting when I got here.

What makes your forehead so smooth and high?
A soft hand stroked it as I went by.

What makes your cheek like a warm white rose?
I saw something better than anyone knows.

Whence that three-cornered smile of bliss?
Three angels gave me at once a kiss.

Where did you get this pearly ear?
God spoke, and it came out to hear.

Where did you get those arms and hands?
Love made itself into hooks and bands.

Feet, whence did you come, you darling things?
From the same box as the cherubs' wings.

How did they all just come to be you?
God thought about me, and so I grew.

But how did you come to us, you dear?
God thought about you, and so I am here.

George MacDonald

WHAT BECAME OF THEM?

He was a rat, and she was a rat,
  And down in one hole they did dwell,
And both were as black as a witch's cat,
  And they loved one another well.

He had a tail, and she had a tail,
  Both long and curling and fine;
And each said, "Yours is the finest tail
  In the world, excepting mine."

He smelt the cheese, and she smelt the cheese,
  And they both pronounced it good;
And both remarked it would greatly add
  To the charms of their daily food.

So he ventured out, and she ventured out,
  And I saw them go with pain;
But what befell them I never can tell,
  For they never came back again.

THERE WERE TEN IN THE BED

There were ten in the bed
And the little one said,
"Roll over, roll over!"
So they all rolled over
And one fell out.

There were nine in the bed
And the little one said,
"Roll over, roll over!"
So they all rolled over
And one fell out.

There were eight in the bed
And the little one said,
"Roll over, roll over!"
So they all rolled over
And one fell out.

There were seven in the bed
And the little one said,
"Roll over, roll over!"
So they all rolled over
And one fell out.

continued on next page

There were six in the bed
And the little one said,
"Roll over, roll over!"
So they all rolled over
And one fell out.

There were five in the bed
And the little one said,
"Roll over, roll over!"
So they all rolled over
And one fell out.

There were four in the bed
And the little one said,
"Roll over, roll over!"
So they all rolled over
And one fell out.

There were three in the bed
And the little one said,
"Roll over, roll over!"
So they all rolled over
And one fell out.

There were two in the bed,
And the little one said,
"Roll over, roll over!"
So they all rolled over
And one fell out.

There was one in the bed
And the little one said,
"Roll over, roll over!"
So he rolled over,
And he fell out.

There was no one in the bed,
So no one said,
"Roll over, roll over!"

FRENCH CRADLE-SONG

If my boy sleep quietly,
He shall see the busy bee,
When 't has made its honey fine,
Dancing in the bright sunshine.

If my boy will slumber,
Angels without number
Will draw near, so fair and bright,
For they only come at night.

If my boy lie still in bed,
God, too, will be pleased and glad,
And will say, "I'll send to him
All night long the loveliest dream."

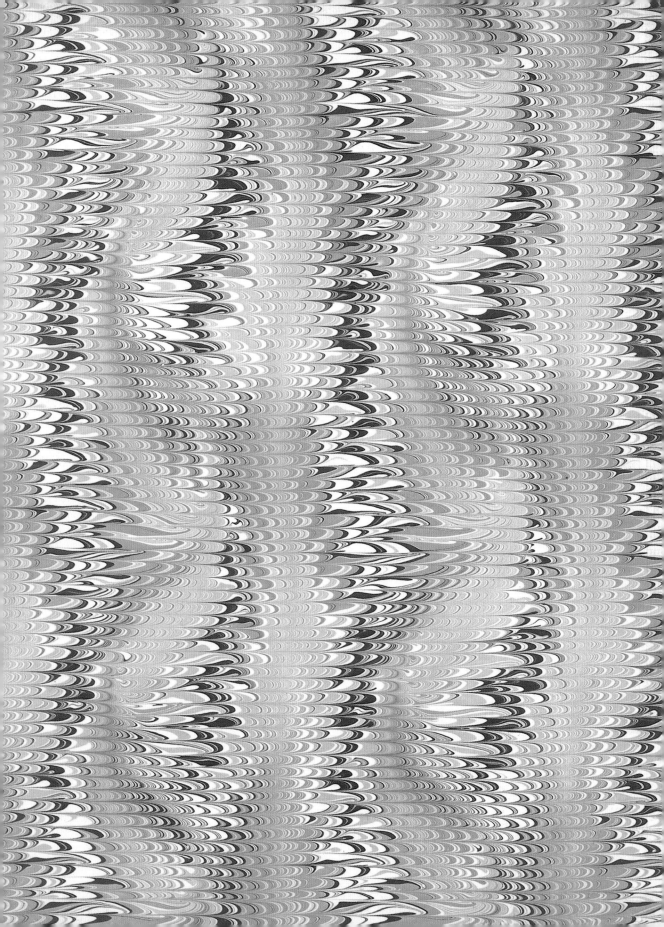